The Dead Past

KATE AARON

Copyright © 2014 Kate Aaron

All rights reserved.

Cover by Elizabeth Mackey Graphics

ISBN: 1499259417
ISBN-13: 978-1499259414

This is a work of fiction. Any resemblance to actual persons, living or dead, is entirely coincidental.

CHAPTER ONE

Tea, toast, strawberry jam. It was the same breakfast Hugo Wainwright took each morning. He rose every day at the first insistent ring of his alarm clock, closed the lever over the clapper, and touched the two brass bells atop the greying white face to stop the hollow, residual echo of the chime. They vibrated a little as he pressed his finger pads against them. His fingertips were smooth, his hands uncalloused save for a lump of hard skin on the side of his third finger, where his fountain pen rested as he wrote. After a quick douse with a flannel and cold water, he dressed in a white vest, blue shirt without collar or cuffs, a brightly knitted pullover, and dark green corduroy trousers with suspenders, well worn and comfortable. The pullover was a Christmas gift, knitted by old Mrs Andrews during the war, before her eyes got too bad for her to see by lamplight during the blackout. The colours were garish, but she had spent a good portion of her rationing coupons on the wool, and Hugo felt churlish for disdaining it. He wore the pullover as a reminder to be more grateful, to please old Mrs Andrews when he went of an evening to read to her, and to add a splash of colour to his black and white newsprint life.

On this particular morning, after rinsing his breakfast dishes, Hugo put on his overcoat and boots and proceeded out into the crisp air of what was to become a beautiful mid-autumn day.

Working as the Arts and Literature correspondent for the *Gazette*, a respectable publication with a small but respectable readership, had many advantages, chief amongst them being the freedom to spend his time as he pleased. Hugo had submitted his latest article the previous day, and had plenty of time before him in which to read his next assignment and formulate an opinion. He therefore felt no guilt as he strolled through the lanes and streets of Puddledown, greeting townsfolk and neighbours with a cordial tip of his flat cap.

Main Street was busy with housewives and harried mamas, and Hugo quickly changed his path, taking a quieter backstreet that ran behind the bakery and butcher's shop and haberdasher and greengrocer's, up through the town and out again into the surrounding countryside of the south of England.

The fields were mostly bare so late in the year; the soil churned and hardened into haphazard troughs and peaks. The occasional green of a ripening cabbage harvest or the tall stems of Brussels sprouts added a splash of oily colour to the washed-out landscape, gaunt trees stretching splayed limbs skyward through the slowly lifting mist.

Hugo pulled his overcoat closer, rubbed his hands, and thrust them deep into his pockets alongside a stubby pencil, a coin or two, half a paper bag of mints, and a screwed-up hanky: the detritus of a man without a wife at home to make him empty his pockets, as his mama had done when he'd been a little boy.

A small flock of geese flew overhead, their strange honking call sounding oddly flat and muted in the damp and misty air. To Hugo's right, the hedgerow rose, its myriad twigs crisscrossed and laced higher than his head, obscuring his view of the fields and, beyond, the shingle-roofed houses of the town. To his left, the road dipped into a gully Hugo knew in spring would be filled with rushing water, before rising again where the first trees of the woods stood bare and isolated from their brothers, Nature's pioneers.

Hugo examined them as he passed, noting their peeling bark, the occasional fallen branch, and here a whole trunk leaning haphazardly against its neighbours. As winter rolled in and the winds got up, some would fall, mighty giants slain with a deafening crack and a groan of limbs, roots snapping, hauling the very earth in their wake. Such was the nature of things.

The forest belonged to the local manor house, managed by a groundskeeper and maintained, as it had been for centuries, to encourage the pheasants and other game the local lord hunted in season with his lofty friends. Hugo crossed the road and entered the woodland, following an ancient path that gave right of way through the forest and would bring him home in a looping five or six mile amble.

The path would cross right by the groundskeeper's cabin, fallen into disrepair over the long, bleak years of the war, when young men had been needed on the Front and not tending His Lordship's game. The last time Hugo had passed this way, it had seemed some improvements had begun: the door was freshly painted, new shingles nailed to the roof, and curtains hung in the windows once more. Hugo had gathered from this that a new groundskeeper had at last taken up residence, although who the man was, and from whence he'd come, Hugo did not know. Never one to listen to idle gossip, if the townsfolk had mentioned a new arrival, Hugo hadn't heard.

There was nobody visible at the cabin when he passed, although he took a moment to look around and shout hallo. Groundskeepers woke early, Hugo reasoned, and judging by the thin plume of smoke drifting from the cabin's chimney, the fire was well on its way to dying down. No doubt the man had been out doing his job since before the sun had come up.

Shrugging, Hugo moved on.

The forest was quiet, many of the songbirds having left already for warmer climes, and those that remained were no doubt silently watching Hugo stride past, the hard ground crunching under his stout boots, his breath swirling in smoky plumes around him. Hugo liked to be fit. A pudgy child, for whom sports had been a torment, he had walked and run off the puppy fat in these very woods, and listened with horror to his mother's tales of life in London, where she had lived for a spell with his papa, a city so steeped in dirt and sin that to tread its streets was to invite robbery. One stepped outside clean and glowing but returned black and grey with soot and smoke.

He rarely walked through the woods these days—in hunting season it wasn't safe, for a start—but he enjoyed the tranquillity on this fine, misty morning, the way the fog shrouded the path and made it seem as though he was the only soul alive and abroad, sauntering through a landscape of shadowy ghosts.

Hugo popped a mint into his mouth, enjoying the sharp burst of flavour and the hard clack of the sweet against his teeth. He whistled a few tuneless notes for the sake of hearing them flatten and fade in the dead air.

A splash of colour on the ground between the trees caught his eye, and he paused, looking carefully at the spot. A reddish smear on a trunk just off the path, that he would have dismissed as a discolouration of the bark were it not for the blue and white paisley pattern of a scrap of material lying sodden on the hard earth beyond it, jumped out at him. Crunching the mint nervously, Hugo stepped off the path, startling as a twig cracked underfoot, the sound like a gunshot, shattering the silence of the woodland.

He paused, listening. The hairs on the back of his neck rose, his palms sweating. He rubbed them against his corduroy trousers. It was a scrap of material, he reasoned as he continued his approach through the eerily silent forest, his skin crawling as he imagined a thousand eyes upon him.

He saw the hand first. Bone-white with blue blotches, fingers clawed, the nails seeming freakishly long and inhuman. It was a small hand, Hugo noted, feeling oddly detached. It was like the whole world slowed and tilted sideways and, if asked later, Hugo would say it was as though he didn't inhabit his body in that moment but was above it, floating somewhere in the bare canopy of the tree branches, looking down on himself as he looked down on that hand.

The hand was attached to an arm, clad in a tweed overcoat which seemed too big and bulky for the frail form it contained, and the arm led to a body: a small body, light, contorted at the oddest angles, like a broken, discarded doll. The paisley was a headscarf, Hugo now saw, hanging in tatters around a face frozen in the rictus of death, its mouth open in a final, eternal scream.

Hugo's gorge rose and he staggered back, a shaking hand over his mouth as his stomach heaved, sending him into a fit of dry retches. He stood trembling for long moments, trying to calm his thundering heart and queasy gut while his brain pieced together what he had seen.

A blue eye, cloudy with cataracts, glazed and fixed in wide astonishment. A lined face, elderly, skin which in life would have been papery and marbled with bluish veins now chalk-white and waxy. Long wisps of grey hair, threaded with silver. A bun, perhaps, untangled in a struggle. For surely there must have been a struggle. The old woman had not come to these lonely woods to die, of that Hugo was certain. Scratches on her exposed wrist, the torn headscarf, and the ugly, gaping wound in her chest attested to the fact her death had been a violent one.

Hugo had only seen one dead body before. His mama had passed badly enough, taken by a fever that produced hot and cold sweats, shakes, and a hacking cough. For day after endless day, Hugo had watched her disintegrate before him, one piece of flaking skin, one gob of mucus at a time, until there was nothing left but an empty husk and a death-rattle that seemed to go on and on.

Yes, his mama's death had been bad enough, but nothing compared with how this woman had met her grisly end.

Moved now by empathy—for the body had once been alive, and not so long ago: someone's friend, or wife, or mother—Hugo approached again, fighting down the rising tide of nausea from his roiling stomach. He knew very little about death, about the decomposition of the human body, but the corpse was intact and seemed frozen stiff, although as a result of rigor mortis or simply a night exposed to the elements in the wintry woods, Hugo couldn't tell.

He should get help, he realised. There was a small police station in the town. One of the local constables could take over, could offer Hugo a soothing cup of sweet tea and ask clipped, businesslike questions about the discovery.

A fresh panic overcame Hugo as he realised he hadn't worn his wristwatch, didn't even know what time it was. What would he say when the constable asked him the simplest of questions? What would they think when he didn't know the answers? Would he look guilty? And what if—Heaven forbid—he ran all the way to the town, brought the constable back to the woods, and couldn't find the body again? The pathway had few distinguishing features, the bare forest like a warren, a maze of never changing scenery. How would he ever find this exact spot again?

Hugo took a deep breath, trying to calm down. He was an intelligent man, a sensible man. The logical thing would be to leave a marker on the path so he could be sure of the location. If only he had worn his woollen scarf! He fumbled in his pockets, groping for anything that could be of use. He thumbed a large copper penny, the old notion of placing coins over a corpse's eyes to pay the ferryman occurring to him. The stuff of superstition, of course, and besides, he couldn't touch the body. Hugo at least knew that.

He was still fumbling in his pockets when the silence of the forest was broken by a slow scraping sound. Hugo froze, all the hairs on the back of his neck rising once more, listening as the strangely metallic *scrape, scrape* moved closer.

Palms slicked with cold and nervous sweat, Hugo took short, shallow breaths, and hoped the thunder of his heart was not audible through his sensible layers of winter woollens and overcoat. The sound moved closer, an irregular, unearthly thing, and Hugo's imagination ran riot, conjuring the shining sickle of Death himself, scratching a path through the bare branches of the trees.

The mist swirled through the woods in a confounding eddy of movement and shadow, separating here to reveal only the silent, unmoving trees, and thickening there to the density of a body, a misshapen body, dark and malevolent. And still the sound came closer.

A swirl of fog to Hugo's right made him start, half-turned towards the path to flee, an alarmed cry lodged deep in his throat. At the last instant he recovered, recalled that grown men didn't scream and run from imaginary terrors, and held his ground, hypnotised by the darkening shadow of a figure, grotesquely outlined by a shaft of sunlight streaming through the canopy behind it.

The shadow moved closer until Hugo could discern the shape of a man about his own height, maybe an inch or two shorter. Not a big man at all. Slim of frame, although broad in the shoulders, their breadth emphasised by the square cut of a thick wax jacket edged in leather. The man wore a dark cap pulled low over his face so all that was visible to Hugo was a granite jaw peppered with two or three days' growth. His hands were surprisingly slender, the fingers long and almost delicate, although roughened and calloused, tobacco-yellowed, and blotchy red in the cold air.

The scraping sound, Hugo now saw, was caused by a shovel the man dragged carelessly, bumping and catching the sparse undergrowth and the hard-packed ground. It slid over an exposed rock and there—*scraaaape*—was the sound that had caused Hugo's heart to thunder so. But the man also dragged something else, something even more terrible than a shovel in the woods on a cold October morning, for in the same hand as the shovel he gripped the drawstring of a hessian sack, seeping and stained with blood.

Hugo's terror rose to fever pitch as the figure advanced towards him—towards the body hidden in the cold, lonely woods, where nobody ever went—and just as Hugo was about to pass out or run, the man looked up, paralysing him with his black-eyed stare, with eyes as black as sin.

CHAPTER TWO

"Bloody hell." The man dropped his twin burdens of sack and shovel, his hands flying to his chest as he released a bark of laughter. "You startled me!"

"I'm sorry." Hugo didn't know why he was apologising. The habit had been ingrained though a lifetime of being polite, being cordial. Now here he was, apologising to a murderer for interrupting his task!

"Nobody ever comes here," the murderer said, picking his shovel up and stepping closer. "You must be the first person I've seen in the woods since I arrived."

"Stay back!" Hugo found his voice and retreated a step, away from the advancing madman. He had no way of knowing if the psychopath was armed, but he was wielding a shovel. What more weaponry did he need?

The man halted, a puzzled expression crossing his face. He would be a well-enough looking chap under other circumstances. Hugo reckoned him to be only a few years younger than himself: mid-twenties, maybe, his skin still tinged with the last of a summer tan, the colouring of a man who worked outdoors come rain or shine. Medium brown hair in need of cutting stuck out from under his cap, and his eyes weren't black, Hugo saw now, but a deep,

deep brown, with barely any contrast between iris and pupil. Fathomless eyes, they were, fringed with long, dark, almost feminine lashes. On another face they would appear so for certain, yet they suited this man, softening features which otherwise, although handsome, would have seemed too severe: his Greek nose, too strong and proud for conventional tastes; his hard cheekbones; and his lips, thinned and pinched as though he bore the worries of the ages on his young, broad shoulders.

Those lips twisted, a sardonic grin that rose in tandem with a single dark eyebrow. "I'm Tommy," the man said, not moving a muscle closer. "Tommy Granger, the new groundskeeper. I should probably tell you you're trespassing." The last said with a smirk.

"It's a public right of way," Hugo said automatically.

"Not off the path, it ain't. An' it's easy enough to get yourself lost in these woods."

"Is that what happened to her?" Hugo asked stiffly, indicating the body, which lay in a small gully between them.

"To who—oh." Tommy had taken a step forward and halted, his dark eyes narrowed as he raked over the corpse. "What did you do?" he asked, his voice calm and even, and icy cold.

"Me? I, I did nothing!" Hugo spluttered. "I just found her and I assumed, well, you're the one carrying a shovel through the woods!"

"A sh—?" Tommy stopped, his features twisted for a second, then he released a long laugh. "There's foxes in the bag." He kicked the sack. "His Lordship took the hounds cub hunting yesterday. You must have heard the horns?"

Hugo nodded slowly. The sound of the hunt had been unmistakable, and although the season proper wouldn't start for another month, it wasn't unusual for new hounds to be trained on juvenile foxes through the autumn.

"Have to bury 'em," Tommy continued. "They attract

scavengers otherwise, and scare off the other foxes. Been out all mornin' collectin' bodies."

Hugo wrinkled his nose. He had grown up in the countryside, but he had no taste for blood sports. Slowly, the wider implications of Tommy's words dawned on him. "So, if you didn't kill her, and *I* didn't kill her...." He looked again at the body, and quickly away.

"How long's she been dead?" Tommy asked curiously, moving closer.

"How should I know?" Hugo asked defensively.

"You mean you can't tell?" Tommy looked surprised. "What kind of war did you have?"

Of course, he'd been a soldier. He must have seen his fill of death, must have studied the decomposition of corpses through every stage of the process. Watched men die, no doubt, and watched the greedy earth slowly reclaim their flesh.

When Hugo and his mother listened to the wireless as Chamberlain made that terrible announcement, back in September of '39, Constance Wainwright had wailed, a slow, keening sound, and clutched her then twenty-two year old son to her bosom and made him swear—*swear*—never to enlist. Already out of university, Hugo had wondered if he would be able to keep that promise, but when the local schoolmaster enlisted to do his duty, Hugo was able to take his place. His war was spent managing unruly children—more than he would have believed possible before the evacuees began to arrive—with too few staff and even fewer resources. With the return of their old master, newly decorated owing to some matter of personal heroism on the battlefields of Europe, Hugo had happily surrendered the reins and withdrawn from schoolteaching forever.

He wondered frequently if not fighting made him a coward, if he could have fought, if he would have survived. Hugo didn't like to admit those misgivings and so said nothing, taking a step back and observing as

Tommy made a cursory examination of the body.

"It's a bad business, all right," he said, retreating to stand at Hugo's side. "She's probably been out here all night, although not much longer by the look of things. Do you know who she was?"

Hugo nodded slowly. As his initial shock and revulsion faded, he'd been able to examine the corpse less as an object of horror, and more as a person. In life she'd worn a bun, that supposition had been correct, although her expression distorted her features and made her less recognisable, a terrible waxwork effigy of the woman he'd once known. "Mrs Fairchild," he said with a grimace. "I'm sure of it."

Tommy's face fell. "Not the old woman from the church?"

"You knew her?"

Tommy nodded. "Not well, mind," he hastened to clarify, "but I always seemed to run into her whenever I went to town. Tried to get me to go to church."

Hugo smiled. That sounded like Mrs Fairchild, all right. Meddlesome at times but her heart was in the right place, and she seemed to have been on a one-woman crusade to save the souls of Puddledown. She'd often got on at Hugo in the past about not attending church on Sundays.

His mother had wanted him to go into the clergy, become a vicar like his father, but he had no ecclesiastical leanings, felt no affinity with the man in the faded sepia photograph he knew as "father" but whom he had never actually known, and increasingly, as the years passed and he matured into a quiet and withdrawn young man, he felt such a career would not only be unsuitable, it would be hypocritical of him to pursue.

He stopped attending sermons at the small stone church, and stopped caring what the townsfolk made of his absences. His Sunday mornings were spent instead on long walks on fine days, or else reading the latest novels, re-reading old favourites, or plinking out a clumsy melody on the old, out-of-tune piano in the front parlour.

Mrs Fairchild did the flowers before services, baked scones for the summer fetes, and organised the jumble sales. The Women's Institute and, during the war, the Women's Voluntary Service, had said her services were "indispensible," whatever that meant. Hugo usually gave her domain a wide berth, and he hadn't laid eyes on her in months.

"Well that settles it," Tommy said. "The old gal was alive and kickin' yesterday morning, that much I can tell you."

"You saw her?"

"Saw her?" Tommy laughed. "She near enough chased me up Main Street, wantin' me to give her some advice about her roses. Took me back to her house and gave me enough cake to feed an army."

Hugo nodded. That was Mrs Fairchild all over.

"We should fetch help," Tommy continued. "Can't leave her lyin' out here like this."

"I was about to," Hugo said, a trifle defensively. "I'll run down to the police station—"

Tommy shook his head. "I'll go to the Big House." He meant Crowe Hall, the local manor, home of his employer. "They've got a telephone up there. It'll be faster."

"You think I should stay here?" Hugo asked.

Tommy nodded. "It's best you do. No telling if we'd be able to find her again."

And with that he was gone, melting into the mist as swiftly as he'd arrived. With Tommy's absence, the silence crept in, encircling Hugo and the corpse of old Mrs Fairchild. Hugo wanted to turn his back on the gruesome thing, but a niggle of superstition refused to allow it, as though he were afraid, deep down, her cloudy eyes would blink and slowly, inexorably, she would revive and crawl closer behind his back.

Instead, Hugo found himself studying her. It was only natural, he reasoned, to be curious. He hadn't wanted to look at his mama's body, hadn't wanted to see her waxy, wasted figure, once so full of life, lying like a statue before him.

There was nothing statuesque about poor Mrs Fairchild. Mr Oliver, the undertaker, would have a devil of a task to make her presentable. The rigor mortis would pass, Hugo knew, but would that mean all her limbs relaxed? Lying as she was, she would never fit into a coffin, and her face demanded a closed casket, at least. Then again, not all people could pass quietly and respectably in their beds, eyes closed and palms crossed over their chests, waiting to be lifted and packed neatly into a box in which to spend all eternity. How was it accomplished, that illusion of order and serenity in death? Were bones broken, were parts tied down and others strapped, lips sewn shut and pallid skin made presentable with powder and rouge? It was the last lie we told ourselves, Hugo reflected, a final token of comfort offered—not to the deceased, but to those they left behind.

From there, Hugo's thoughts turned to his unexpected companion in disaster. Tommy had hardly glanced twice at the body, as unmoved in the presence of death as Mr Oliver himself. Of course, Tommy had been in the war, just like every other young man except Hugo. Had it been cowardice on his part to have stayed—had he done it not to alleviate his mama's fears, but his own? He had only occasionally fired a gun, being neither a rich boy from a country seat with hunting in his blood, nor a farm lad with livestock to protect. His mama had kept a few chickens to give them eggs and meat for the pot, but even in a place as unassuming as Puddledown the ration hit hard, and none of them had survived the war. Then, afterwards, Constance had fallen ill, and Hugo had never seen fit to restock the disused coop. He missed their cheerful clucking most of all.

Tommy was younger than Hugo, yet in the cruelties of

life he seemed infinitely more experienced. Obviously not a local, his accent spoke of the Thames, though not of London itself. Tommy was a country boy through-and-through, a man used to living his life in the open air, schooled in the ways of the birds and the beasts that shared his isolated forest home. Why would a young man like that seek employment here, of all places? What possible future could Puddledown offer him?

There were girls aplenty in the town, more so since so many of the menfolk had gone to war, never to return. Lasses of eighteen and nineteen, sweetly optimistic for the future, their naivety neither bombed nor starved out of them. Not that Puddledown had ever been bombed. Some incendiaries dropped, once, on a field beyond the old mill, no doubt to lighten the load of a German plane fleeing a dogfight. They had lit up the horizon like a bonfire, like a shower of falling stars, but caused little damage and made even less impression. No, Puddledown had been safe, as safe as anywhere, and mamas from the capital shipped their children to the town for safekeeping until the war was over. Many had returned to city life, but some had stayed. Some had nowhere left to go.

Women, too, abounded, for the young man with interest and a bit of time to spare. Young fiancées who'd lost their fancy men to the Germans, widows with infants in their wake, and plainer girls, lucked out because even the plainest men were able to take their pick. The older ladies of Puddledown shook their heads in sad regret at their daughters' plight, another generation of sons and husbands gone to waste. "Never again, never again," was the constant refrain, ringing out from the pulpit and shop counters alike.

Yet what woman would take a groundskeeper, would choose to live in the forest, far removed from the comfort of town, gossip, and friends? It was an isolated life Tommy had chosen, and icy fingers crawled once more down Hugo's spine as he recalled tales—told in hushed voices, half-overheard, but never reported in the newspapers—of young men gone mad at the Front, of institutions with high stone walls filled with mumbling soldiers still reliving the war. What if Tommy had gone, not for help, but to check the coast was clear, to fetch more weapons with which to dispatch Hugo alongside the corpse of the woman he had murdered yesterday?

But Tommy had seemed neither mad nor dangerous. Just another young man craving solitude as he tried to forget all the terrible things he had seen during the war.

It seemed both an interminable amount of time, and yet no time at all, before the tramp of feet and the sound of voices heralded the arrival of the local constable, escorted by Tommy and, surprisingly, His Lordship himself, Robert Fairfax, Viscount Crowe, owner of the title for which the surrounding borough had been named.

"So what have we here?" the constable demanded in a tone that said he wouldn't believe in the presence of a body until he saw it with his own eyes, even if the call had come from the Big House.

His name was Jimmy, Hugo recalled, Jimmy Cooper, although these days he no doubt preferred James. He'd enlisted early, keen to "do his bit," striding through the streets of Puddledown in his uniform like a regular popinjay whenever he returned on leave. He'd spent his war in France, never making Dispatches but remaining alive and fighting all the same, and if he lived to be a hundred, Hugo doubted he'd ever let anyone forget he was already in the thick of it when the bombs started falling.

Hugo stepped aside and indicated the body, hanging back while Jimmy and Lord Crowe strode forth to investigate.

"Sorry about him." Tommy nodded at His Lordship, speaking in an undertone. "Damn butler insisted on askin' for permission to use the telephone, and once he heard what it was about, he felt 'duty bound' to come along." The way he emphasised the words, Hugo could hear them clearly in his head, picturing the scene, and he shared a guilty smirk with Tommy.

With the presence of a body confirmed, the woodland was soon awash with activity. Hugo and Tommy were shepherded back to Tommy's cabin to await the arrival of an inspector who seemed in no hurry to question them, and contented themselves with watching the procession of official and serious-looking persons on the path leading to and from the grisly find.

"Tea?" Tommy asked at length, opening the cabin door and beckoning Hugo inside.

"Please." Hugo knocked his boots against the door jamb in lieu of a mat, and stepped into the dingy building.

The cabin had two rooms, a stone sink and potbellied stove serving as a kitchen against one wall, a small, rough-hewn wooden table and two chairs before it, and an old horsehair sofa that had seen better days dominating the remaining space, its back to the door, facing a large, bressumer-beamed fireplace. The pipe from the stove fed into the mantle above the fire and must, Hugo thought, have been the source of the thin wisps of smoke he had observed—a lifetime ago, it seemed—when he'd passed by the cabin that morning.

It was with the stove Tommy was fussing now, raking over the embers to heat a small kettle of water placed on its flat top. The bare floorboards creaked as he moved around the tiny space, setting out a pair of mugs, a jug half-full of milk from a pail beside the sink, and a tiny glass bowl containing that most precious of commodities, sugar. A tin ashtray, a caddy of tea, a small, stained strainer, and a dented spoon completed the ensemble, and Hugo took the seat Tommy indicated with a curt nod of his head, removing his cap and running a hand through his shock of fine, sandy hair, suddenly nervous and wishing he'd had the foresight to tame it with Brylcreem before leaving his house.

Hugo was not a social creature. In company, his anxiety

got the better of him, led him to imagine everyone else was judging him, finding him wanting. It was as though they could all see right through him, like the sins of Hugo's soul were written plainly across his skin. Not that Hugo was a sinner. Even within the sanctuary of his own mind, he tamped down on lustful, impure thoughts, thoughts that turned him crimson to the tips of his ears, at once aroused and deeply, profoundly ashamed.

Being around others made Hugo feel ashamed, and here, doubly so. There was something too intimate about Tommy's cabin, about its utter lack of pretension. It made Hugo feel ostentatious and wasteful, having a whole house to himself. The closed door at the far end called to him: Tommy's bedroom, Hugo was sure of it. Was it as sparse as the rest of his home, or had he marked his personality on the space, hung a painting or lined up sepia photographs of somebody—his mama, his brother, or a girl he once knew—upon a sturdy dresser? For, despite the Spartan accommodation, Tommy's personality was evident everywhere in small, homely touches. In the bright woollen blanket laid carefully along the back of the sofa, in the dark, masculine curtains hung over the windows, and in the somewhat unexpected addition of a small sprig of holly in a jam jar on the centre of the table.

Tommy placed the tea strainer over the first mug, added a spoonful of dried tea leaves, and picked up the kettle as it started to whistle. Both mugs filled, the amber liquid slowly swirling and infusing, Tommy took the chair opposite Hugo and pushed the milk and sugar towards him with a half-bashful smile and a nod.

Hugo helped himself to milk, but left the sugar untouched. It was generous enough of Tommy to offer, without him being so greedy as to accept.

"Have some," Tommy insisted, nudging the bowl closer when Hugo pushed it away. "You had a shock this morning, an' nothin' soothes the nerves like sweet tea."

"I couldn't possibly—" Hugo protested, but Tommy

had already taken a heaped spoonful and dumped it in his mug.

"There." Tommy laughed. "Now you'll have to."

Hugo shook his head, chuckling ruefully as he took up the spoon and began stirring. The first sip was heaven, he couldn't deny it, and the satisfied look on Tommy's face as he watched him drink assuaged the last of Hugo's guilt.

"What about you?" Hugo asked, nodding at Tommy's unsweetened drink. "You didn't see anything I didn't."

"I'm all right." Tommy shook his head. "Nothin' I haven't seen before."

"But you knew I hadn't." Hugo set his mug down. "How?"

Tommy ran a hand up the back of his neck, ruffling his untidy hair. "Couldn't say," he answered gruffly. "Just don't seem the type, is all."

"What type?" Hugo persisted. "The type to enlist, to be a soldier, to see a dead body without—" Without, what? Without being afraid, without jumping like a skittish colt at every crack of a twig or sound of another living person approaching? Shame washed over him, scalding hot.

"It's all right." Tommy touched Hugo's wrist, squeezing briefly through the layers of overcoat and shirtsleeve before retreating, leaving only the impression of warmth in his wake. "I didn't mean nothin' by it."

"It's me." Hugo smiled sadly. "I'm too sensitive. But you're right, for what it's worth. I never did sign up."

"Then you're lucky," Tommy declared. "How'd you escape war service?"

"Schoolteacher." Hugo grimaced. "They tried to get me. In the town, I mean. Said I ought to enlist. My old man died in the First War, before I was born. Mama begged me not to go."

His father had been a rector, from a long line of men of God. Not a fighting man, but a padre, his duty and calling had been to offer comfort to the poor devils bogged down in the muddy fields of France, or at least send them on their way with a few decent words to guide them. Nobody told the Germans Ernest Wainwright was a man of God and, as with so many others in that terrible wasteland, the war proved Ernest first and foremost a man, and the soft ground around the banks of the Somme swallowed all men just the same.

Tommy nodded, dark eyes wide with understanding. "Wish somebody had begged me not to," he said, then took a long swallow of tea, hiding his face.

A rap at the door made them both start, pushing their chairs from the table and rising guiltily, the same way Hugo remembered the boys at Dorchester Grammar used to when the Housemaster entered a room. In the doorway stood, not some learned figure in cap and gown, but a portly, middle-aged man sporting a felt hat and long trench coat belted at the waist.

"Misters Granger and Wainwright, I presume?" The man consulted a small notebook and needed no further introduction to mark himself as the expected inspector.

Hugo and Tommy nodded.

"Detective Inspector Owens. George Owens. Has anyone spoken to you gentlemen yet?"

Hugo and Tommy shook their heads in unison.

Inspector Owens snorted with something like irritation. "We'd best get started then. If Mr Granger wouldn't mind waiting outside...?"

Hugo bristled at Tommy's abrupt eviction from his own home, but Tommy left without a word of complaint.

Hugo's questioning didn't take long, for he really had very little to tell. The inspector seemed most interested in his account of Tommy's arrival upon the scene, and Hugo was annoyed all over again at the wheedling insinuation in the inspector's tone, his own earlier suspicions long forgotten.

His tale told, Hugo was dismissed and Tommy summoned, in a process so familiar from Hugo's schooldays he half-expected to look down and see his knees protruding from short trousers, greying socks bunched untidily around his ankles. They exchanged schoolboy smirks at the doorway before carefully stepping around each other, an awkward do-si-do as Tommy entered and Hugo exited the cabin. Unsure if he was free to leave or not, Hugo took a seat on a rough bench alongside the cabin door which, he now noted, Tommy had failed to fully close. The low murmur of voices drifted out in a lulling rhythm, soothing Hugo as he waited.

The sun had finally emerged, burning off the morning mist, and the woodland seemed a beautiful place, with the soft yellow light dappling the ground through the branches. The superstitious horror that had gripped him that morning seemed an alien sentiment, a far cry from his staid, sensible nature and quiet way of life.

Already the memory of the experience was fading, like the things he had seen were just the details of a disturbing picture show from a daytrip to Dorchester or Weymouth: the images, so shocking at first, proving perhaps too shocking to ever thoroughly absorb.

More voices, this time from the direction of the path, focused Hugo's attention on a slow, careful procession emerging from the trees. Hugo rose and, realising he'd left his flat cap on Tommy's table, bowed his head, hands clasped before him in a last gesture of respect as Mrs Fairchild, her remains shrouded in suitably sombre black, was carried from her shallow grave back towards the small town where she had spent her life.

It was an ignoble end for a woman who had lived her life well, had done all the right things, gone to church and said her prayers and put her faith in a higher power, trusting that goodness would be rewarded. *Some reward*, Hugo thought bitterly. To die a painful death out here in the forest, without a measure of comfort or solace, no priest to say the right words, no family to hold her cold, papery hands, nobody to hear her screams....

Hugo shuddered, aware suddenly of his own mortality,

the indiscriminate hand of death looming large over all of them. If Mrs Fairchild, of all people, could meet such a terrible end, what lay in store for poor outcasts like Hugo? He was long resigned to a life of celibacy, without comfort of a wife and children as other men had. He had thought himself accustomed to the idea, even if he could never be wholly content with his lot, but now, pondering his eventual demise, Hugo couldn't help but wonder if he wasn't punishing himself too severely.

Hugo didn't hold with the notions of Heaven and salvation the way the rest of the townsfolk did; he had no faith in a benign God who would reward him in another life. Once he was gone, Hugo expected nothing more than for his flesh to feed the worms, his bones turn to dust, and the lettering on his modest gravestone to weather and crumble until there was nothing left of him at all. No evidence that Hugo Arnold Wainwright had ever walked the earth.

Yet, it was human nature to believe the worst, to remain superstitious about Hell and damnation long after faith in God had been lost. Perhaps it was foolhardy to deny his nature out of fear of cosmic reprisal, but then again, Hugo considered, as Tommy and the inspector emerged from the cabin to join him in his silent salute to the fallen woman, perhaps even now he was being tested.

Hugo returned Tommy's small, furtive smile as the inspector looked the other way, and admired the way the groundskeeper's dark eyes shone in the morning light. He didn't believe in God, or the Devil—not really—and he didn't believe he was being tested, but Hugo couldn't help but think, as he schooled his features into something more befitting the sombre occasion, that if meeting Tommy was a test, he was about to be found sorely wanting.

CHAPTER THREE

In the days following his discovery in the woods, Hugo did his utmost to return to his usual routine. He woke each morning with the first alarm, ate his usual breakfast of tea, toast, and strawberry jam, read the book he was supposed to be reading for the *Gazette*, and did his best to close his ears to the gossip of the ladies at the shop counters in Main Street.

What he did not do—what he absolutely did *not* do—was lie awake at night, his thoughts returning again and again to the grisly sight of that broken, bloodied body, to the gaping chasm in her chest, to her wide-mouthed, eternal scream. And if he should wake with a start in the small, cold hours before morning, the reverberation of an entirely new scream still ringing in his ears, he simply shrugged and turned over, and most certainly found no comfort in thoughts of the strangely enigmatic young woodsman with whom he had shared the discovery.

Thoughts like that had led him to London, to places spoken of in hushed tones or scorning voices. They had kept him awake through long, lonely nights at university and, earlier, even at school, as boyhood admiration turned to puppy love and more.

Hugo knew exactly what sort of man he was, and exactly what the world thought of men like him. He had remained in Puddledown precisely to avoid such temptation—such hopeless, deviant temptation—ordering his life instead around a simple routine, simple pleasures. Tea, toast, and strawberry jam.

But Hugo was nothing if not a sensible, rational man. Although unassuming in air, he possessed great intellect, and he turned his curious and analytical mind inward now, reasoning through his sudden change in circumstance, after a lifetime of carefully nurtured self-denial.

It was the shock, obviously. It was not every day a man found a body in the woods. His careful mask momentarily stripped away, his defences down, was it really surprising he'd latched onto the first decent soul who'd crossed his path? A man who remained calm in the face of disaster, who took charge and said the right words to assuage Hugo's terror, and his shame at feeling terrified? He had been vulnerable, and Tommy was simply there at the right moment, with the right words. Hugo thought he would probably have fallen a little bit in love with practically anybody who would have rescued him that morning.

Thus Hugo reasoned and rationalised his responses, turning them over and over as a taxidermist studies a specimen, looking for the perfect place to make the first incision, to take the remains of a living thing and immortalise it: an insect trapped in amber. So Hugo would etherise his emotions, splayed and displayed in the locked cabinet of his mind: once-living things, warm and vital, now reserved for the dry dust of a scientifically curious gaze.

Finally, one morning in the week following Hugo's ill-fated walk through the woods, it happened. The last of the jam ran out.

Hugo had known the day was coming. For some time now he had been rationing the jar with ever-decreasing helpings, small, crumb-encrusted scrapes of drying jelly picked out from under the rim with the edge of his knife. Eventually, however, even the most determined soul must admit defeat.

The jam had been sour, made with over-ripe fruit from the garden and too little sugar by his mother during the summer of '45, just after the war had ended and before the fever carried her off. He hadn't touched it in the longest time. It sat on its shelf in the pantry, a silent sentinel in wax paper, a ring of grease forming around the string as the years went by. To Hugo, the jam had resembled her optimism, her faith in a future in which there would be sugar and fruit to spare, time for the jam to mature, and many mornings on which to eat it.

Hugo lovingly washed the jar and returned it to its rightful place in the pantry. The shelf was marked where it had sat, a lighter ring on the dusty, whitewashed shelf. He touched the spot, a fond smile on his solemn face. The last tangible link to his mother was gone, and it felt like he ought to mourn her all over again, wrap the jar in black crepe as a mark of respect.

Recognising he was about to get maudlin, Hugo wiped a hand over his face, closed the pantry door, threw on his overcoat, and left the house, the stout front door closing behind him with a rattle of the letterbox.

The first frost had arrived a day or two earlier, and Hugo exited the house and entered a sparkling world of shimmering white. The frost adorned every surface, glittering like diamonds where it caught the light of the early morning sun. The slate roofs of the chocolate-box cottages in Hugo's lane were dusted with white, their small, square-paned windows reflecting flashes of liquid gold as Hugo trod the uneven cobbled pavement.

Puddledown had been as far removed from London as his mother could possibly get. Newly widowed, with a squalling babe-in-arms, she had fled the capital and all the memories the place held for her. In 1917, single women with babies had been a shockingly common sight, and not all were as innocent as his mother. She had moved three times before landing on Puddledown, where she found employment as a nurse at the Big House, tending the scores of wounded soldiers brought back from the Front.

Hugo breathed deep the crisp country air. He had been to London, and understood better his mother's aversion to the city. It was not as dark, dirty, or dangerous as she had claimed, but he had known instantly that cities were not for him. The sheer size of London, its myriad, teeming streets, the noise and frantic energy of the place, had shocked him.

The only thing Hugo missed about the city was its anonymity. The people of London hadn't called him *Poor Hugo*, or remarked that already, at thirty-two, they could clearly see the octogenarian lurking within. "Old before his time," the folk of Puddledown said, with sad and rueful shakes of their heads. They thought him strange; a queer child who had grown into a queerer man.

He saw few people until he had walked as far as Main Street, but whereas he would usually shy from the gossiping women in the shop queues, this morning Hugo wanted to hear other people, normal conversations, the small details of mundane lives.

The general store was already a hive of activity, the ladies of Puddledown convening early to discuss the weather, the ongoing ration, and the rising price of sugar. Hugo joined the back of the line, head down and hands in his pockets as he patiently waited his turn at the counter and tried not to eavesdrop on the other patrons.

Hugo had no time for gossip, thinking there was something distasteful and a little bit cruel about knowing all the details of a stranger's life, raking over their triumphs and disasters as though the cares of others were nothing but fodder for idle speculation, supposition, and disdain. An intensely private man by nature, it perturbed him to think others felt entitled to the minutiae of his life by virtue of geographic proximity alone. He might live amongst these people, but he was not, and had never been, one of them.

The bell over the door chimed as another customer entered the shop, and Hugo's heart sank as Mrs Ponsonby barged past to join a group of woman standing before him in the queue. The curate's wife, Mrs Ponsonby was the self-appointed leader of the ladies of Puddledown, a prominent member of the WI, the parish council, and numerous other local committees. She had been, if not a friend, then a close colleague of the late Mrs Fairchild, which made her about the last person Hugo wished to see.

Unable to escape without drawing further attention, Hugo kept his head down and his cap pulled low, hiding his face in the upturned collar of his overcoat as best he could. He cringed as the conversation immediately turned to the arrangements for Mrs Fairchild's funeral, due to be held later in the week. The cause of death had been a single deep stab wound to the chest, probably delivered from behind, and executed with skill and precision. This much Hugo knew from the write-up in the local newspaper, which had covered the murder and doctor's report in lavish detail.

What had concerned him was the implication, emphasised by the reporter, that the killer was a man trained to deal in death. Tommy's presence had been mentioned, but Hugo rejected the thought that the groundskeeper could have committed such a terrible crime.

The women had also obviously read the newspaper, because they were discussing the case openly, speculating as to the identity of the murderer within their midst as if the brutal death of one of their friends and neighbours was nothing more than a plot point in a Saturday picture show.

"You know who found her, don't you?" Mrs Ponsonby said, the varnished berries on her felt hat clacking as she nodded.

"Hugo Wainwright?" A woman farther down the queue

half-turned to answer. "He always was a queer boy. It doesn't surprise me in the least that he was involved somehow."

"Mmhmm." Mrs Ponsonby pursed her lips. "And that new groundskeeper was with him, so they say. I ask you, what would a quiet man like Hugo Wainwright be doing in the woods with a ruffian like him at the crack of dawn? They were clearly up to no good."

Hugo's blood froze in his veins and he wished he was invisible, that he could flee before he heard what else the too-observant ladies of Puddledown speculated about him. Guilt crawled down his spine and settled in his gut, despite his sins never having been committed, not even in the darkest, most secret corner of his mind.

"I always said he was a wrong 'un," the other woman said with a long sniff.

"Who, Mr Wainwright?"

"No, that groundskeeper. Gardener or Granger or whatever he calls himself. A young man like him, all alone in the woods like that. It's just not right."

"Well, you heard about the day she died?" another woman said, joining in.

All the ears in the store pricked, and even Mr Ledbetter, the shopkeeper, paused to listen.

"Came into the town, he did. The groundskeeper. Looking like he'd been pulled backwards through those woods of his. But Mabel didn't mind, not her. Well you know she was a charitable soul, and she was looking for some advice about her roses. 'Go to the Big House,' I told her, 'the gardener'll see you right.' But she saw that groundskeeper and thought he might be able to help. Though, between you and me, I think what she really wanted was to talk to him about the church. Never been to a service yet, he hasn't, and Mabel always was a good, God-fearing woman."

All the women nodded thoughtfully and bowed their heads for what they deemed a respectable length of time before the original speaker continued, surrounded now by a rapt audience.

"Went after him, she did. Told him she wanted his assistance and wouldn't take no for an answer. Then she,"—the women leant closer—"she... oh, it's too awful to contemplate. She invited him back to her house, and nobody saw her alive again!"

"No!" Shocked gasps sounded throughout the store.

The woman nodded vigorously. "It's true, I swear it as God is my witness."

"And you've told the police?" Mrs Ponsonby enquired.

"Of course. Spoke to that nice Inspector Owens."

The ladies nodded, satisfied.

Hugo's heart was pounding. He hadn't thought Tommy a killer. A part of him still didn't. He couldn't reconcile the laughing young man who'd insisted on him taking a spoonful of sugar with his tea with the calculating, cold-blooded way Mrs Fairchild had met her end.

That Tommy appeared to be the last person to have seen her alive was no indication of guilt. Yet Mrs Fairchild was known by all as a kind soul who wouldn't harm a fly. Hugo couldn't imagine anybody wanting to murder her. Tommy was a stranger, a young man with a murky past, and by his own admission he had been alone with her just before she died. Her body had been found beside his cabin.

A tendril of doubt curled around Hugo's heart, curdling his insides. Tommy he had been at that place, out of all the hidden places in the woodland, carrying a shovel and a blood-stained sack which, Hugo realised with a sinking heart, he had only Tommy's word contained the corpses of fox cubs. It could have been anything in there—bloodied clothing, incriminating evidence, even the murder weapon itself!

Blood rushed in Hugo's ears, drowning out the sound of the gossiping women. That they were talking of him was bad enough, but to associate him with a murder, and such a grisly one, was a thought too awful to contemplate. He, Hugo Wainwright, a man who blanched at killing a chicken for the pot, to be thought of as capable of... of....

He had to get out. The store was too warm, stifling, the snooty ladies with their idle gossip and haughty ways and wide wicker baskets and the decorative fruit on their hats clack-clack-clacking like gunfire around him, raking over his life like he was a story in a newspaper, a character in a novel, and not a man who had lived for thirty-two years amongst them, played with their children, tipped his cap to them in the street.... It was too much. Far, far too much for any man to bear.

The women gave startled gasps as Hugo emerged from the cocoon of his cap and coat and turned to flee. That they hadn't recognised him was evident in the expressions of surprise and guilt on their faces, but as Hugo barged out of the store, their chagrin didn't prevent a final annoyed admonishment about his manners following him out the door, punctuated by the cheery tinkle of the bell as it swung closed behind him.

Hugo walked blindly up Main Street, shying away from anyone who passed too close, blind and deaf to their greetings and shocked exclamations alike. He reached the end of Main Street and kept walking, out onto the lanes surrounding the town and up through the empty fields beyond. He didn't slow his pace until he was approaching the woodland once more, a decision now needing to be made.

He could turn around and walk back through the town, but the thought of facing those people again made him sick to his stomach. He could continue along the lanes and arrive home by a circuitous route some ten or twelve miles long that would take him the rest of the morning and a good deal of the afternoon to complete, or he could confront his demons head on by taking the shortcut through the forest, past the place where all his recent troubles had begun.

THE DEAD PAST

Hugo hesitated for only a moment before veering off the lane onto the old footpath through the woods.

Macabre, maybe, to want to revisit the site, but he had questions that needed to be answered and he hoped, in lieu of the police arresting the culprit and securing a full and frank confession, he could set his mind at ease and, if nothing else, prove he could walk this way again.

The woods looked very different to the day on which Hugo had found the body. A steady procession of feet had marked the path, flattening the sparse growth at either side to make a wider thoroughfare, more clearly defined than Hugo ever remembered it being before. The mist, which had added an eerie, otherworldly aspect to that morning, had lifted, it being now well into the day, and with the sun shining and a few birds singing, it was altogether a different forest into which Hugo now strode.

He had not walked half the distance to Tommy's cabin when a cheerful whistling halted him in his tracks. Unless he was much mistaken, Hugo recognised the opening melody of a popular tune from the wireless, something sad and melancholic about waiting for love, and before he could stop himself he had whistled a few notes in return.

Tommy—for it could only be Tommy, working in the woods somewhere out of sight of the path—paused a second, then a more cautious, exploratory burst of notes floated through the trees. Smiling, Hugo stepped off the path and through the undergrowth in search of the groundskeeper as he picked up the sad, sweet melody and continued the refrain.

The crackling of twigs sounded as Tommy also approached, materialising through the trees from out of a deep gully hidden from the path. The two men paused, grinning as they finished the last few bars of the chorus, then laughed before greeting each other.

"Didn't think I'd see you here again," Tommy said. "Thought last time would've scared you off for good."

"That might be partly why I'm here," Hugo admitted.

"I like these woods. Always have. Didn't want one bad experience to put me off."

Tommy tipped his head, dark eyes focused inquisitively. "An' the other part?"

Hugo blushed. "It hasn't been easy," he admitted. "People in town, they gossip, and I don't like being spoken of at the best of times."

"Ah." Tommy nodded, his expression showing a touch of sympathy. "Like that, is it?"

"Just needed to clear my head," Hugo mumbled, wondering why he'd started this conversation. Why hadn't he continued along the path and left Tommy to whistling and working in peace? Why bother the man at all, when clearly the last thing he needed was some bumbling fool who'd seen a body and now couldn't sleep at night disturbing him. Tommy certainly seemed to have no problem being alone in the forest.

Suddenly, Hugo felt mortified all over again.

"Anyway, I'd best let you get on—" He half-turned towards the path, but halted when Tommy demanded he stop.

"Why don't you help me?" Tommy suggested. "I'm tryin' to clear out a stream before the plants grow up in spring an' block it, but I could do with another pair of eyes to point me where I'm going."

"You're sure?" Hugo asked, the suspicion surfacing that Tommy was only humouring him to be kind, a second suspicion following that he'd accept the offer anyway if it meant he didn't have to be alone.

Tommy shook his head and beckoned for Hugo to follow as he vanished from view back into the gully.

Hugo found to his relief there was some truth to Tommy's words. The "stream" was little more than a glorified drainage gully, emerald green with moss on the lower banks, sloping down to a trickle of muddy, sluggish water. Hugo could see how easily it would stagnate in summer if the plant growth wasn't curtailed, and he spent a diverting hour calling out directions to Tommy, who wielded a sharp-bladed shovel with aplomb in the silt below.

Between them, they soon had a clear channel cut through the worst of the moss and reeds, the banks scraped clear of plant growth for a good foot or two on either side, and Hugo cheered to see the slowly trickling water pick up pace and move with some purpose downhill to where it would eventually merge with the River Crowe.

Tommy scrambled up the bank, smiling and mud-splattered, and Hugo felt no awkwardness at all informing his new friend of his ghastly appearance.

"Tea?" Tommy offered, handing over the shovel and laughing as Hugo took it, then suddenly realised he'd been relegated to common labourer. "It's 'bout time you got those nice hands of yours dirty," Tommy said, elbowing Hugo's ribs, smiling so good-naturedly that nobody, and certainly not Hugo, could possibly have taken offence.

CHAPTER FOUR

Back in the cabin, Tommy set the tea things and a battered tin ashtray on the table, and wiped the worst of the mud from his face and arms with a damp cloth. The holly was gone; in its place in the centre of the table were a few tall sprigs of strongly scented yarrow, the clusters of small white flowers brightening the place.

Tommy had clearly shaved some time since Hugo had last seen him, although not in the day or two immediately prior. Hugo found he liked Tommy's beard scruff, which was a shade or two lighter than his hair and highlighted with bright, almost ginger tones. There was something so devil-may-care about it, neither a full beard nor Hugo's neat, clean-shaven countenance. Shaving was a chore Hugo would happily forsake were it not for fear of censure from the scandalised women of the town, and his mama's constant refrain that a man with a beard was usually hiding a weak chin and weaker nature.

Tommy's chin didn't seem weak to Hugo. Rather, it appeared as strong and compact as the rest of his frame, neatly squared with a small dimple just visible in the centre. Tommy's beard growth extended beyond his chin, down his neck to his Adam's apple. Hugo averted his gaze as Tommy wiped the damp cloth into the open neck of his collarless shirt, exposing a strip of milk-white skin the sun obviously never saw.

Dropping the cloth into the stone sink, Tommy took the shrieking kettle from the hotplate atop the stove, filled both mugs, and sat. The two of them helped themselves to milk and sugar as though they had done so many times.

"So the whole town's talkin' about us?" Tommy asked conversationally, lighting a cigarette as he waited for his tea to cool. "They saying anythin' interesting?"

Hugo hesitated, but the ironic arch of Tommy's eyebrow shamed him into speaking frankly. "They say we killed her," he said in a rush, blowing on his tea and taking a scalding gulp that made his eyes water.

"What?" Tommy's eyes widened with astonishment. "Why ever would they think that?"

Hugo fussed with one of the yarrow sprigs but stopped when a handful of flowers came loose and fell. "Because you were seen going to her house...."

Tommy released a bark of laughter. "That don't make me a murderer." He took a long drag of his cigarette, thoughtfully blowing the smoke away from Hugo when he exhaled.

"No, of course not." Hugo retreated hastily from any hint of accusation.

"Here, you don't honestly believe I done it?" The sudden concern that crossed Tommy's face, as though Hugo were both judge and jury, moved him. He barely noticed Tommy's hand on his wrist until it was gone, leaving only the cool impression of having been touched. The ghost of a sensation, no more. "Because I didn't. I swear. I mean, I know it don't look good, me being there all alone, plenty of opportunity, as they say, but men have harmed me worse than that old gal ever did an' they've all lived to tell the tale. I never hurt a soul if I could help it."

"I believe you," Hugo said, finding as the words left his mouth that they were true. Maybe it was naivety on his part, but he simply couldn't imagine Tommy attacking an old woman, struggling with her, plunging a knife between her ribs and wrenching....

Hugo shuddered. No, definitely not.

"Well, good." Tommy curled his hands around his mug, slow tendrils of cigarette smoke rising between them. "I don't even hold with blood sports, me. I saw enough death in the war to last me a lifetime."

"Where were you based?" Hugo asked, curious now Tommy had brought it up. Some men wouldn't let you forget they'd served, boasting to any who'd listen of the places they'd been and things they had done. Others were quieter, unwilling to discuss the time they'd spent in service, wishing the whole experience away like it was a bad dream they just wanted to forget. Hugo knew his interest was macabre, given he'd never served, but he had always wondered, as he heard the tales the men brought back from the Front, if he could have done it, if he would have survived, and he was endlessly curious about the men who had.

"France," Tommy answered, his voice devoid of emotion, his eyes growing dull and flat.

Hugo nodded. Most of the menfolk in the town had served on the Continent, just across the thin strip of the English Channel. A hop, skip, and a jump from home, yet a whole other world, it seemed. "What was it like?" he asked, leaning forward, an avid expression on his face.

Tommy levelled him with a long look. "It was Hell on earth," he said, stabbing the butt of his cigarette viciously in the ashtray. "Any man who says he weren't scared is a liar. 'Specially if he was at Dunkirk."

"You were at Dunkirk?" Hugo gasped. He had followed the story, as much as the newspaper censors would allow. The routing of the British army by the German forces, the retreat to the beaches of northern France, the flotilla of private boats and naval warships that had between them rescued over three hundred thousand men and returned them home, safe and sound, ready to fight again. It had been a stirring enough story, even before Mr Churchill's rousing speech about fighting on the beaches and never surrendering.

"Don't make it sound like a bloody holiday," Tommy groused. "There were thousands of us. We thought we was going to die, mown down right there in sight of home. Some fellas made a swim for it, but those currents are strong. Six hours, I waited for a boat to pick me up. Six hours in water up to my neck. I thought I wasn't never going to get rescued."

"I'm sorry," Hugo said, immediately contrite.

Tommy shrugged. "I were one of the lucky ones, in the end. Got saved after all."

"You, you knew men who weren't?"

"Didn't everyone?" Tommy snapped. "It's best forgotten, now. We won, an' they say that's all that matters."

"Your experiences matter," Hugo said softly. "What you went through... but you're right. I won't ask anymore."

"Drink your tea." Tommy's voice was gruff but, despite himself, Hugo grinned as he lifted his mug.

"What about afterwards?" he asked after a short silence. "You didn't stay in the army?"

"Heck, no." Tommy shook his head vigorously. "Got my discharge and stayed in London for a while. Seemed like every sapper and tommy who'd got his papers was there."

"Is that why they call you Tommy?" Hugo asked, suddenly making the connection. Tommy the tommy.

"Aye. That, an' my name's Thomas." Tommy smirked. "Never suited me, though. I were only Thomas if I were in trouble."

Hugo smiled. He'd never had a nickname or abbreviation, but as a child, on rare occasions when caught misbehaving, he'd suffered the full wrath of *Hugo Arnold Wainwright*.

"Anyhow, London got too busy for me, too many fellas and not enough work, even with the Olympics goin' on, an' I reckoned I had nothing keeping me there, so I left."

"What about where you came from?" Hugo asked. "You never thought of going home?"

Tommy shook his head. "Nothing left for me there. My pa died back in '44, never saw the end of the war. Ma moved to live with my sister in Scarborough. She didn't want me around."

"Why not?"

Tommy shrugged and, just for a second, Hugo got a glimpse of a much younger man, bright with vitality and optimism. "Her old man's a vicar. Thinks I'm the heathen sort."

"And are you? The heathen sort?"

Tommy gave a bashful grin. "Mebbe."

Hugo laughed. "My father was a vicar," he said. "He died before I was born, though. I'm something of a heathen myself."

"You are?" Tommy's grin widened and he sat a little straighter, appraising Hugo afresh. "You don't look the type."

"Haven't been to church since I was seventeen," Hugo said with some pride. "Except for Mama's funeral, that is. Can't say I ever really bought into the whole Hell and damnation bit."

"You think you're going to Hell?" Tommy asked curiously, his tone softer. "Why?"

Hugo blushed. "No reason. I reckon that's where everyone ends up, according to that book. We're born sinners, aren't we?"

"An' you don't regret your sins?" Tommy's voice was low, purring, his dark eyes pinning Hugo to the spot. "You don't believe you can be saved?"

Hugo got the distinct impression they were talking at cross-purposes, although he couldn't divine the hidden meaning behind Tommy's words. To cover, he blustered, gulped his tea, and prayed for Tommy to change the subject.

"In my book, it's all a lot of rot," Tommy said, rescuing him. He spoke louder, the soft, insinuating tone gone from his voice like it hadn't been there to begin with. "But that's why I don't see our Beth, any road. Her chap wouldn't have me hanging around. So I moved west instead. My old man was a gamekeeper, an' I reckoned there must still be one or two houses where things were run how they was in Pa's day, an' eventually I landed up here."

"Do you like it?" Hugo asked, half-covering the real question he wanted answering. *Do you intend to stay?*

"Oddly enough, I do." Tommy laughed. "Even after what we found last week."

"Yes." Hugo shuddered. "I hope that doesn't happen again. It's usually so quiet around here."

"You're from here, right?" Tommy leant forward, elbows resting on the tabletop, which tipped slightly in his direction. "How come you never got out?"

Hugo contemplated his mug of almost-finished tea. He could have left Puddledown, of course he could. There had been a time he'd considered doing so. But the wider world held temptations Hugo didn't think he had the fortitude to withstand, and then there had been his mama.... "I thought about it," he admitted. "It just never seemed to happen."

"Well, it's nice enough here," Tommy said. "Certainly for a country nothin' like me."

"You're not nothing," Hugo said hotly, surprisingly himself with his vehemence. "That is... I mean...."

"I understand," Tommy said softly. "An' thanks."

Hugo flushed.

"So, you don't have many murders here?" Tommy kicked back in his chair, arms behind his head, elbows spread wide. It took Hugo a second to realise he was half-joking.

"No," he chuckled. "Not many. I've lived here all of my thirty-two years, and this is the first I've heard of."

"You can't think of anyone who might have done it?"

Hugo contemplated the question. It wasn't everybody who could wield a blade with such force and precision, even on a frail old woman. The butcher, perhaps, but Hugo didn't think ruddy, cheerful Mr Fletcher had the constitution of a cold-blooded killer. Then again, he realised with a sinking heart, practically every man in the town between the ages of twenty and sixty had some kind of military training. Even Hugo had been in the Home Guard.

"There's enough capable," he finally said. "But I can't think of any who would have a motive. She could be a meddling old soul, true, but is that any reason to kill somebody?"

"I wouldn't have said so." Tommy shook his head. "But there must have been someone thought different."

The thought sat uneasily with Hugo, that the townsfolk of Puddledown might even now be rubbing shoulders with a murderer.

"It could have been an accident," he reasoned, although it felt like he was clutching at straws. "Say she saw something she oughtn't...."

"Like what?" Tommy prompted.

Hugo considered. "A robbery, perhaps? If she disturbed some villain—"

"Has there been a robbery?" Tommy interrupted.

Hugo's shoulders sagged. "Not that I know."

"An' why dump her in the woods?" Tommy wondered aloud, picking up the thread of the mystery. "It's quiet enough, there's that. If you hadn't happened along, she could have lain there for months. But it's a long way from the town to bring a body, an' anyone could have spotted him along the road. It was quite a chance to take."

Hugo liked the sound of this less and less, but he couldn't deny his analytical brain was interested in the mysterious circumstances of the murder. If not Tommy—and Hugo was as sure as he'd ever been of anything that his new friend wasn't a killer—then who, and how, and why? The culprit seemed to have gone to a great deal of trouble to attack and kill an old woman, then move her body through open lanes, only to dump her in the woodland, barely ten feet from the path. Surely, if the purpose of leaving the body in the woods was to prevent its discovery, it would have been prudent to place it farther in, in the deep, dark places where people seldom trod. By the time Tommy or the hunt stumbled over the remains the killer could have been long gone, all his tracks covered, and the body so decomposed a cause of death would never have been determined.

But no, Mrs Fairchild would have been missed from the town long before such a time, and the cold ground and colder air would act as a preservative. There would have been a search organised, within the town at first but then assuredly it would have spread, out into the lanes and farmland and, eventually, the woods. It would have been nigh on impossible for the body to simply disappear, reclaimed by the greedy earth.

There must be something, Hugo felt sure, some vital detail he had overlooked, the key that would unlock the mystery. Old ladies simply didn't get stabbed and dumped in woodlands, at least not in Puddledown. No, Hugo was certain there was some deeper riddle here, some underlying motive he had yet to divine. And, he admitted, as he watched Tommy rinse their mugs and toyed absently with the sprays of sweet-smelling yarrow, he couldn't deny he was intrigued, both by the circumstances of Mrs Fairchild's death, and by the curious young man with whom he'd shared the discovery.

CHAPTER FIVE

The folks in town were still talking about the murder when Hugo made a return trip to Main Street the following day. He could have avoided them, he supposed, but he was running low on almost everything, and it seemed a cowardly thing to do, to take a bus to the next town over simply to buy a few groceries. Hugo had lived in Puddledown his entire life, and he wasn't going to let the gossips drive him out now.

Plus, he found he was much calmer, fortified against the townsfolk since his conversation with Tommy. He'd spent several hours with the groundskeeper, ruminating on the identity of the killer and the strange details of the case, before the lengthening shadows had prompted him to take his leave. Tommy had escorted him through the woodland, past the place where they had discovered the body, and Hugo felt eternally grateful he hadn't had to walk by that spot alone. They had paused long enough at the edge of the forest for Hugo to point out the neat row of slate roofs, one of which was his, before going their separate ways once more.

The small brass bell over the door of the general store tinkled as Hugo entered. The shop was quieter this morning, it being a Wednesday and the deliveries arriving on Mondays—a fact Hugo had overlooked the day before. He tipped his cap to Mr Ledbetter and the two ladies at the counter, and took a moment to peruse the tinned and household goods on the shelves opposite. He selected a new bar of Pears soap and joined the short line to await his turn to pick over the meagre offerings available.

From the general store he went to the butcher's and the greengrocer's, where he ran into the vicar's wife, who reminded him Mrs Fairchild's funeral was to be held on the morrow, and surely Hugo would be there? Unwillingly, Hugo assented, more to wipe the horrified look from her face than because he felt any obligation to attend. Appearances were everything in a small town like Puddledown.

Prior to going to bed, Hugo laid out his single black suit, bought secondhand in the days before his mama's funeral and stored in mothballs ever since. He polished his black shoes until they shone and then polished them a second time for good measure, before fretting that their high shine now seemed too jaunty for such a sombre occasion. Finally, after much to-ing and fro-ing, succeeding only in annoying himself, Hugo left the shoes as they were, gave up the idea of fashioning a black crepe armband, and went to bed.

The morning broke cold and damp, it having raining during the dark hours of night, and Hugo noted with glum resignation, as he took a seat on one of the old wooden pews at the back of the nave, his shoes were mud-splattered and scuffed from his walk into town and all his efforts the night before had been for naught.

Reverend Brown, the vicar, was still standing at the church doors, welcoming all who entered with a press of damp, limp hands and a few sombre words of welcome. Words which, in Hugo's case, had risen in an exclamation of surprise and pleasure, the crescendo dying in a gentle chastisement for his long absence, and an enquiry when

Hugo would see fit to rejoin the flock. Hugo had muttered something noncommittal in response, but couldn't help feeling Tommy would have had both the words and the nerve to rebuff the man more thoroughly.

A decent-enough chap of middling age, Reverend Brown had taken over when the previous incumbent, Reverend Pottle, had at long last been called to meet his Maker at the ripe old age of seventy-two. Reverend Pottle had been the priest of Hugo's childhood, a fire and brimstone man who much preferred the Old Testament to the New. The Reverend Brown, by contrast, seemed a far staider cleric, never much of one to get involved in anything more taxing than the dates of the jumble sales or praising the ladies' flower arrangements, leaving matters requiring greater diplomacy to his wife, the very capable Edith, who had so neatly annexed Hugo in the greengrocer's the previous day.

The Reverend kept the service brief, for which Hugo was grateful. He owned a dark sort of disappointment that the casket was closed, its high-polished wooden top bedecked with a spray of winter flowers, no doubt gathered by the church ladies from their hothouses for the occasion. A sole relative sat on the front pew, a man of advancing years whom Hugo assumed to be a younger brother or cousin of the deceased, both her children having succumbed to influenza in the months following the First War.

Hugo stopped listening to the sermon after the first prayer. He had heard it all before, at his mama's funeral, and had no wish to relive the experience for the sake of someone who, after all was said and done, was almost a stranger to him. Instead he looked around the church, admiring not for the first time the grand old edifice, the earliest wing of which dated back to Norman times, or so they said. Constructed of weathered red sandstone, slate-roofed, with an imposing bell tower at the north end, it was an impressive sight both inside and out, certainly for a town as unprepossessing as Puddledown. Dedicated to St. George, its stained glass window on the south wall bore a striking mural of the slaying of the dragon, the mighty beast clutching a spear lodged deep in its throat while above it, the Saint's white steed reared and kicked its hooves. There was no sign of the distressed damsel in the scene, but then Hugo didn't suppose the story was really about her, anyway. The sun flashed through the coloured panes as it tracked across the sky, throwing rainbows of light down onto the dull stone pulpit below.

He had buried his mama in the churchyard, a small ceremony held in remembrance of a small, unassuming woman from a small, unassuming town. He had visited her grave once a week at first, as that seemed most appropriate for a dutiful, loving son. He'd brought her flowers from the garden and tidied the grasses that in spring grew tall enough to obscure her simple headstone, but eventually he realised nobody was watching him, nobody keeping track, and his visits languished to once a fortnight, once a month, then stopped altogether.

To the sombre notes of organ music, the coffin was carried at the head of the slow procession of townsfolk out into the churchyard to the freshly exhumed grave of the late Mr Fairchild, where Mrs Fairchild would be laid to rest, flanked by her children. Not so much time had passed that the letters of the weathered stones had become illegible, and Hugo read them now. "Annie Fairchild, Beloved Daughter. 1901-1919" and "William Fairchild, Beloved Son, 1903-1919." *For we are the children of God.*

Somewhere near was his mother's grave, although Hugo studiously avoided looking in that direction, as though, if he looked, her neglected headstone would reproach him for his long absence; as though her very ghost would rise up and demand to know why he had forsaken her. The dead had no lives on their own. It made sense they would try to suck life from the living.

A few words said, a few handfuls of dirt thrown, and

the funeral party left the open grave for the diggers to close and returned to the front of the church to mill in small groups and pass the time of day, albeit in hushed voices, for it was still a solemn occasion.

"I say, you will be coming to the inn, Mr Wainwright? Mr Rourke has put on some sandwiches."

Hugo viewed the invite with trepidation under the watchful, slightly avid gaze of a handful of the ladies. He had hoped to avoid any sort of wake and mistakenly assumed, as Mrs Fairchild had been elderly and had no relatives to speak of, there wouldn't be anything planned for him to avoid. A hopeless fancy, he now realised, with the dead woman being the only victim of a murder in Puddledown's living memory.

Unable to think of a suitably convincing excuse in time, Hugo was swept along with the rest of the townsfolk towards the local inn, the Crowe Arms. The landlord, Mr Rourke, was already standing behind the pumps at the high bar, pulling pints of pale, frothy ale and rich stout to order.

Tommy would've got out of this, Hugo thought glumly as he accepted a cool, dimpled glass of amber liquid, a slick of foam running down the side. Tommy *had* got out of it, shunning the funeral and the town entirely. Safe in his cabin in the woods, he probably didn't even know the funeral had been held. Hugo found himself in the odd position of feeling envious.

Thinking of Tommy, however, turned Hugo's mind to the subject of their last conversation: namely the motive and identity of the killer. Realising the townsfolk might have their own thoughts on the matter, Hugo took a bracing gulp of ale and proceeded to join in the nearest conversation.

He soon wished he hadn't. First there was Mrs Ponsonby, retelling the tale, overheard in the general store, of Tommy going with Mrs Fairchild to her house on the morning she died, although the story had been embellished almost beyond recognition, with Tommy now all but chasing the venerable old lady down Main Street with the murder weapon in hand.

Then there was Mrs May from the bakery, deep in conversation with Jimmy Cooper, the police constable, and Jimmy was telling all within earshot how, if *he* had command of the case, he'd have arrested that no-good groundskeeper already, locked him up, and thrown away the key.

Turning with distaste from the pompous bobby, Hugo bumped straight into Mrs Goodwin, one of the church ladies, almost slopping his drink down himself in the process.

"Oh, I do beg your pardon—why, it's Mr Wainwright, I do believe. How *are* you, my dear?"

Hugo nodded stiffly at her enquiry, trying to subtly remove his arm from her surprisingly firm grip.

"I heard you found poor Mrs Fairchild, God rest her soul. And thank Heaven you did! The very idea of her lying out there, in those cold woods...." Mrs Goodwin gave a delicate shudder. "It quite chills the blood."

"As you say, I'm just happy she was found," Hugo mumbled, not adding he rather wished it had been somebody else doing the finding.

Mrs Goodwin dismissed his words with a flick of her hand, pulling him closer, away from the press of people surrounding the bar and sandwich table. She lowered her voice conspiratorially, and Hugo had to incline his head to hear her. "They tell me you saw him, as well."

"Him?"

"The groundskeeper! The one they say done it. They say you caught him burying her body—right in the act!"

"That's not at all true," Hugo said, standing straight and extricating himself from her grasp. "Tommy happened by afterwards, entirely by accident."

"But you've heard what they say about him, surely? Oh, I know you're not one for gossip, Mr Wainwright—and nor should you be, nor any of us—but one overhears things...."

Hugo struggled to refrain from rolling his eyes, although he couldn't help but wonder what else the townsfolk had heard of Tommy's past.

"... from London, they say he is. Oh, not originally, mind, though his accent's near enough. A more uncouth young man I never did see. Run off, he was, by his family. That's how he wound up here. Couldn't go home, see? They say his own father were the one to do it."

"That's simply not true," Hugo interrupted, bristling at the blatant slight on his friend's character. "Tommy's father died during the war."

Mrs Goodwin's eyes narrowed. "Know that for a fact, do you? Or did *he* tell you?" She took a step back, drawing herself up until they were almost on eye level with each other, all her limbs straight and taut. "I must say, Mr Wainwright, you seem very pally with him all of a sudden, given he's the suspect in a murder inquiry. 'Tommy,' is it?" She sniffed. "At times like this, it's best to remember who our friends really are."

"As I assure you, I do," Hugo replied, equally haughtily. "And whatever you may have overheard in taverns"—he gestured towards the red-faced policeman—"Inspector Owens has given me no indication Tommy is anything other than a witness to an unfortunate crime. Until such a time as I hear otherwise from a *reputable* source, I intend to refrain from listening to idle gossip. I bid you good day."

With that, Hugo placed his half-full glass on the nearest tabletop and strode from the inn, struggling to keep his smile contained until he had at least left the building.

He felt like running home, like unbuttoning his overcoat and holding the corners out like wings as he soared down Main Street, as sure and righteous as a Spitfire. He felt like whooping for joy, or else surrendering to a fit of boyish giggles. *He had put one of the church ladies in her place!* He could barely give credence to the thought.

Hugo did none of those things, of course. He thrust his hands deep into his coat pockets, buttons fastened against the chill air, and strode down Main Street at a more sedate pace, although still brisker and bouncier than was his wont. At first he had been curious about—and mildly appalled by—the promise of salacious details from Tommy's past. To hear the blatant falsehood repeated as gospel had been a much-needed tonic. The townsfolk knew nothing about the murderer, and even less about Tommy.

Hugo hugged the thought close, a warm feeling rising in his chest. Only he understood, only he had taken the time to get to know Tommy, to extend a hand of friendship and hold an actual conversation with the man. Only Hugo appreciated Tommy or saw him as he really was. The rest of the town, isolated and inbred, saw only a stranger in their midst, and looked no further than his unshaven face and mud-splattered clothes to the kind and generous soul who resided within. Would a murderer offer a shaken stranger a spoonful of sugar in his tea or walk a grown man through a darkening forest so he didn't have to tread the path alone? Hugo sorely doubted it.

No, Tommy was no killer, just a folk-devil conjured by the townspeople because it was more convenient to blame a stranger than to look deeper into their own midst. How foolish they would all look when the true culprit was finally unmasked!

Hugo spent a most satisfactory evening imagining first one and then another of the gossiping wretches on trial for the murder, in between attempting to read the latest novel he'd been sent by his editor, and preparing and eating a light supper of a single boiled egg.

As Hugo readied for bed, he realised none of the story had sunk in, and he would have to re-read the last hundred pages on another day if he didn't want his review to be hopelessly confused and rambling. No, rather than absorbing the story—which wasn't, admittedly, all that thrilling, but he had to read nonetheless—his day had been given over almost entirely to thoughts of Tommy's vindication.

A worm of guilt stirred in Hugo's gut. He had only met the groundskeeper twice and, even under such extraordinary circumstances, his interest in Tommy was too keen to be wholly pure.

Hugo knew he was prone to impure thoughts about other men and had long distanced himself from any such temptation, afraid he was too weak-willed to resist on his own. Puddledown was safe, filled as it was with older men, happily married men, or else men with whom Hugo had been raised, who held neither mystery nor attraction for him.

Then there was Tommy. Tommy with his hard, compact body and sinful eyes and milk-white collarbones. Tommy with his easy smile and fleeting touch of Hugo's wrist, his musical laugh and his slow, sardonic humour. Hugo bit the inside of his cheek until tears pricked his eyes in an effort not to remember, not to focus on the way Tommy's slim fingers splayed and ruffled through his messy hair, how his Adam's apple moved in his throat as he swallowed, how he looked when he was hard at work, splattered with mud, the Devil's own smirk on his face.

Tommy wouldn't hold with Hugo's affections for a moment. He had been a soldier, a man of honour, a man who worked the earth and bent it to his will. Such men—such strong, virile men—had neither time nor patience for pallid, bookish types, who pinned all their hopes on two lines of Greek, illicitly translated when they had been forbidden from doing so.

Once Hugo had read those first, shocking lines—not so shocking, he admitted now, at least not in explicit detail—he had craved more, searching out new interpretations and translations of received texts, discovering a world the likes of which he had never dreamed possible: a world in which men could love other men and not be thrown into gaol for it.

Alas, that such a world existed only within the dry and dusty pages of a centuries-old book and would never—could never—exist in England. Hugo might not have been alive when that infamous Irish playwright stood trial, but the shadow of his name stretched beyond the last century and well into this. Hugo had been born three thousand years too late, or a hundred years too early. He was a man caught out of time, suspended in a void from which he could not—dare not—reach out.

CHAPTER SIX

Hugo awoke the following morning determined to turn over a new leaf. Just because he and Tommy happened to have both been witness to the discovery of a murder victim, that didn't make them friends. They had absolutely nothing in common, and it had been pathetic of Hugo to stray into the woods on the offhand chance—he now admitted—of seeing the groundskeeper again. Tommy was a decent, hard-working, salt-of-the-earth chap, and the last thing he needed was some lecherous scholar getting under his feet, hoping for... for... what, exactly? Hugo wasn't entirely sure. All he knew was his desires, shadowy, insubstantial things, made the pit of his belly roll with lusts he had no idea how to act upon, even were he to be given a chance. What could two men possibly do with—for—*to* each other that would not bring the wrath of the whole world down upon their heads?

No, Hugo determined to set thoughts of Tommy aside, to return to his neatly ordered life and live quietly and respectably alone, a confirmed bachelor until the end of his days. His feelings would fade, as they had done before, and the empty keening of his lonely heart would die, suffocated by dignity and routine.

So he began his day, rising with the first alarm, splashing his face and underarms with cold water, reading the newspaper the newsagent's boy had delivered over the top of his steaming mug of tea and two rounds of toast.

Hugo didn't read the local paper, the weekly *Puddledown Press*. He had no time for the petty intrigues of small town life, preferring instead the less mundane news from Dorchester or farther afield, and once a week he treated himself to a copy of the *Sunday Times*, which was delivered on Monday mornings.

He perused the first few pages with little more than passing interest until, halfway down the fifth page, his gaze was inexorably drawn to a small header at the bottom of the inside column. "Puddledown Murderer Detained." Forgetting his breakfast, Hugo pulled the page closer and read on.

PUDDLEDOWN, DORSET. Thursday gone was arrested one THOMAS GRANGER, 27, Groundskeeper for The Right Hon. Viscount CROWE, of Crowe Hall, on the charge that he did, on the 12th inst., wilfully and brutally murder one MRS MABEL FAIRCHILD, 66, widow, late of the aforesaid Puddledown. Granger will be held in police custody until a hearing at Dorchester Crown Court, to be scheduled for a later date.

Hugo's heart leapt to his throat. While he'd been at the funeral or listening to idle gossip in the inn, naively congratulating Tommy for having escaped the tribulations of small town politics, poor Tommy was being taken into custody for a murder Hugo felt sure, in every bone of his body, he hadn't committed.

Without dallying another second he rose from the table, threw on his overcoat, and raced towards the town, the sound of his front door banging closed sounding behind him as he tore up the lane.

Puddledown police station was a small, yellowstone

THE DEAD PAST

building, set square on the corner of Main Street opposite the church. Poor Tommy must have been arrested during the service or after Hugo had left that awful wake. If only he had listened more intently to the words of that bumbling, oafish Jimmy Cooper, perhaps he could have secured Tommy's release before he was forced to endure a single night in the clink.

Hugo was wheezing by the time he ascended the stone steps of the police station and opened the heavy oaken door. Inside, his heart sank to see Jimmy Cooper sitting behind a counter looking a little the worse for wear and clearly still suffering the ill effects of over-indulging at the inn the previous day. Thinking small, mean thoughts about how it served him jolly well right, Hugo took a moment to catch his breath before proceeding to the desk, where he stood, growing more and more impatient as Jimmy made him wait for his attention.

Finally, the constable set his pen down and looked up, a bored expression on his smug face. "How may I help you?"

"Did you arrest Tommy?" Hugo demanded. "Why? You know he's innocent!"

"I'm not at liberty to discuss an ongoing investigation—"

"It's in the bloody newspaper!" Hugo's cheeks heated at the curse, but it was taking every ounce of his self-control not to reach across the desk and shake the constable until his teeth rattled.

"We have taken the culprit into custody, yes. But that's not really any of your business, is it?"

"Tommy wouldn't hurt a fly!" Hugo protested. "You don't honestly believe—"

"Inspector Owens has made a thorough investigation of the matter—"

"Then he got it wrong!" He huffed with frustration, his efforts to remain calm sorely hampered by the malevolent glee he saw dancing in Jimmy Cooper's eyes. Even as boys, they hadn't got along, and Hugo thought he liked the man even less.

"That will be for a jury to decide," Jimmy said. "But for God's sake, man, why do you care? Until you're called to testify—"

"Testify?" Hugo recoiled. "Testify to what?"

"Well, you saw him, didn't you? Coming up to the body all covered with blood and carrying a shovel—"

"What about the knife?" Hugo demanded. "The murder weapon. Did you find that in Tommy's cabin?"

"That's none of your—"

"No, see. Where's that, then, if Tommy did it?" he asked triumphantly.

"Probably buried in the woods, with Lord only knows how many other bodies," Jimmy retorted, rising from his seat and leaning over the desk. "But why do you care, Hugo? What does it matter to you if some groundskeeper hangs or not?"

The blood drained from Hugo's face at the policeman's soft, insinuating words.

Sensing he'd hit his target, Jimmy continued, his voice low, purring with malice. "Hadn't thought that far, had you, Hugo? Granger's going to swing for this, you mark my words. And there ain't nothing you can do about it."

"Let me see him," Hugo asked, the plea squeezed through gritted teeth.

"No."

"*Please*, Jimmy—"

"That's Constable Cooper, to you," Jimmy said sharply. "And I'm not having a witness interfere with the culprit. Not unless you're more than a witness.... Were you in on it, Hugo, is that it? Did the old bag see something she shouldn't have, out there in the woods? You were taking that stroll awfully early...." Jimmy let the accusation linger.

"It wasn't anything like that," Hugo replied, his cheeks burning with shame and anger. "I know he didn't do it—I *know* it. There's a killer out there somewhere, and you're going to let him get away scot-free, all because you're too dense to tell a witness from the villain."

"Now hang on just a minute—"

"You'll see," he said, his voice rising to a decidedly shrill pitch. "I'll prove it, even if you won't. I'll find who really did this and expose you all for the ignorant fools you really are!"

With that, Hugo flounced from the police station, the harsh, braying laughter of Jimmy Cooper ringing in his ears.

CHAPTER SEVEN

Despite his best intentions, Hugo realised, after storming home and brewing a soothing mug of sweet tea, he had no idea how to go about finding the identity of the killer. He was no detective or police inspector, had no training in the art of deduction, and he'd never been able to tell whodunit in any murder mystery he'd ever read. He was an academic, a scholar, his tools merely words written to entertain. He could wax lyrical about Biblical allegory or foreshadowing, but he was at a loss to say where to start solving a real-life crime.

To give himself something to do so he could at least feel he was being useful useful, Hugo took out his notebook. He worked for a newspaper, he reasoned, he had observed enough reporters doing their jobs, and what were reporters if not investigators? Recalling some of his more uncouth colleagues, Hugo swore if they could do it, so could he.

Unscrewing the cap of his favourite pen, he commenced making lists. Lists of facts, lists of suspects, lists of possible motives and holes in the logic of the inspector's cut-and-dried case. It simply didn't occur to Hugo that the police could be right, Tommy could be a killer. It was downright inconceivable.

As dusk fell, Hugo looked over everything he had written, the frantic spider-scrawl of his jumbled thoughts poured out onto the foolscap. It was useless, every last word of it. Hugo couldn't think of a single person in town who made a likely killer, nor a valid reason why they would target Mrs Fairchild and dump her body in the woods. It was completely beyond him.

Disheartened and unable to settle in his cosy house with Tommy facing the certain prospect of a second night under lock and key, Hugo decided to pay Mrs Andrews a call. A widow in her seventies, Hugo had been reading to her once a week or so since he'd returned to Puddledown from university. His mama had worked with the old woman at the Big House back when it was a convalescent home for soldiers after the First War, and the two women had remained firm friends ever since. Mrs Andrews and her late husband had been like an aunt and uncle to young Hugo growing up, and he remained devoted to her now.

She lived two streets down, in a small house not dissimilar to Hugo's. All the cottages were built alike: slate-roofed, two-storeyed, with a parlour, dining room, and small kitchen downstairs, two bedrooms and a bathroom upstairs, a built-in pantry beneath the staircase, and a small outhouse at the back, although most were disused in this modern age of indoor plumbing.

These days, Mrs Andrews was largely confined to the downstairs portion of her home, her bed having been brought to the parlour after arthritis set in and the stairs became unmanageable. A neighbour's girl popped in once or twice a day to check on her, and brought her a hot supper of an evening. Other than Hugo, she had no regular visitors he knew of, and guilt crawled down the back of his neck as he realised it had been almost three weeks since his last visit.

He let himself in with a cheery hallo so she knew she had company. Grace, the neighbour's girl, was just emerging from the parlour-cum-bedroom, a tray containing a mostly empty soup bowl and teacup in her hands.

"Oh, Mr Wainwright, that was good timing. Rose will be pleased to see you," Grace said, neatly sidestepping him to get to the kitchen.

Hugo doffed his flat cap and mumbled a reply before darting into the bedroom the moment Grace's back was turned. She was a bonny lass, must be seventeen or eighteen by now, with a sweet nature and a ready smile, which always made Hugo nervous around her. Grace Kemp was nothing like the gossiping harridans of the town, but now that she was definitely a young woman and not a girl, Hugo was inexplicably tongue-tied around her. Women were an enigma to him, and single women of marriageable age, doubly so. Theirs was one mystery he felt no compunction to solve.

Rose was sitting against a veritable mountain of pillows, her frail form seeming swamped in a voluminous white nightdress, her silvery hair neatly brushed and plaited in a long rope that lay across her shoulder and trailed towards her lap. Hugo had known her stout in comfortable middle age, and that was how he always recalled her best: with flaxen hair just beginning to grey, sporting utilitarian tweed skirts and matching short jackets. During the war, she had been one of the first ladies in Puddledown to take up wearing men's trousers, donning a pair of blue overalls to work around the house and in the garden to the scandal of the neighbours. Mr Andrews had simply laughed, said he'd spent a whole marriage letting her have her way, and he wasn't about to change. Arthur had passed the previous winter, at the grand old age of seventy-eight, and Hugo had mourned him as the closest thing to a father he had ever known.

Rose welcomed him now, her dark eyes cloudy with cataracts but still quick, none of her faculties having deserted her when her body began to go to pieces. "Hugo,

I was wondering when I'd see you again."

"I'm sorry, Aunt Rose." Hugo stooped to kiss her papery cheek before taking a seat in the wingback chair beside her bed.

"Nonsense, boy. I only hope you were away for a good reason. Got yourself a young girl, perhaps?"

"No, Aunt," Hugo said, blushing furiously.

"Give it time." She patted the back of his hand. "You'll meet someone one of these days."

Hugo didn't like to contradict her, and so said nothing.

"So, tell me the news." She settled herself comfortably facing him, her lined face bright with expectation.

"I take it you heard about Mrs Fairchild?"

"I did, but I want to hear it again from you."

Hugo smiled as he began the tale. It shouldn't have surprised him that, bedridden and housebound though she was, nothing had escaped Rose's attention. She probably knew more of Hugo's involvement in the matter than he did himself.

"I never liked her," Rose said with a sniff after Hugo had finished narrating the story. "Always thought she was too high-and-mighty, did Mabel. Obsessed with the sins of others, when I can tell you, she wanted to get her own house in order first. Oh, the things she got up to before she married her Bobbie. They don't bear repeating."

"Aunt!" Hugo gasped, faintly scandalised. "Don't speak ill of the dead."

"Well it's true," Rose said simply. "And don't take that tone with me. You're a man of the world, Hugo Wainwright. Don't tell me you don't know what I'm talking about."

Hugo blushed scarlet but remained silent for, although he had a vague idea, in truth he wasn't a man of the world at all, and didn't pretend to understand exactly what Rose meant. He was thirty-two years old and had never even been kissed. The mysteries of sex were beyond him.

"What are you reading?" he asked instead, hoping she'd

allow the matter to drop.

"Whatever you were reading last time. *Othello*, wasn't it?"

"That's right." Hugo rose to retrieve the small leather-bound book from a pile on the table before the window, pausing to straighten a vase of dried flowers on its doily. Returning, he settled into the chair, cracked open the cover, and found the page he had marked on his last visit.

Rose loved Shakespeare. While he was alive, Arthur had taken her regularly to see the performances the Dorchester playhouse put on, and now in her dotage, Hugo was sure she relieved them as he read to her, seeing once more the characters she knew so well come to life. Clearing his throat, Hugo began to read.

He was generally fond of Shakespeare, and of *Othello* in particular, although he couldn't have said why. He'd always found himself, as a schoolboy, rooting for scheming, devious Iago to triumph, and it had pleased him no end, upon first reading, to discover Iago was not brought to task within the play, but instead the ending was left open, granting the possibility of escape. For the first time, however, the words Hugo read troubled him. As Othello knelt at Iago's feet and swore to him a sacred vow—as Iago, too, knelt and demanded the world witness his returned loyalty and affection—Hugo found himself stumbling.

"What is it?" Rose asked. "I can hardly hear you."

"Nothing, Aunt." Hugo cleared his throat. "I'll start over."

"Oh no, you won't." She smoothed the neat floral counterpane over her lap. "Talk to me. I've heard that story a thousand times. I want to hear something different. Is it this young groundskeeper they've arrested that's bothering you?"

Hugo didn't ask how she'd guessed. Rose had always been sharp as a tack.

"They're going to hang him," Hugo said, his voice

strangled.

"What, he's been tried already, has he?"

"No. But he will be."

"What makes you think he'll be convicted?"

"He was the last person to see her alive," Hugo admitted miserably.

"That means nothing," Rose said with a wave of her hand. Her expression turned inquisitive as she asked, "A nice boy, is he?"

"He's not a boy," Hugo said with a roll of his eyes. "He must be almost my age."

"Ah, you're all boys," Rose said. "Even when you're men, you still act like children."

Hugo smiled.

"What's he like?" she continued. "It's been a long time since I met a stranger around here, and a young man, even longer. Tell me about him."

"He, he's nice," Hugo said, although the word seemed utterly inadequate. "More than nice."

"He was in the war?"

Hugo nodded, then vocalised his answer, not sure she had seen the movement. "He was at Dunkirk."

"A bad business, that."

"Yes, but he got out all right."

"And since then?" Rose prompted.

Hugo shrugged. "He says he was in London for a bit. Left before the Olympics and came here. His dad was a gamekeeper, so he knew the job."

"Lives out in that old cabin, does he?"

"That's right."

Rose sniffed. "I don't blame him. Why, when I was your age, I'd have happily gone and lived out there. Plenty of peace and quiet, no neighbours watching what I was doing, nobody to please but myself...." She nodded, satisfied with the idea. "Yes, he could have done a whole lot worse for himself than wind up there."

Hugo chuckled. "You're the first person who didn't

take it as a sign there's something wrong with him."

"There's nothing wrong with wanting to be left alone," Rose said sharply. "And even if he is a bit odd, that doesn't mean he's a murderer."

"Exactly." Hugo punctuated the word by snapping the book shut. "He swears he didn't do it, and I believe him."

"Then let's think about this," she said, sitting straighter against her pillows. "I always enjoyed a good mystery. Who would possibly have wanted Mabel dead?"

"I don't know," Hugo admitted. "And I don't know where to even begin looking for the culprit."

Rose tutted. "This isn't the Hugo I know talking. I thought you were smarter than this? *Think*, Hugo."

"I can't think of anybody. There's no one in town capable—"

"Murderers don't walk around with signs over their heads," Rose said dryly. "That's why they're so hard to find. They look just like you and me."

"I know," Hugo grumbled, scowling like a child. "But it simply doesn't make *sense* for one of the townsfolk to suddenly decide to start murdering, and to pick on Mrs Fairchild in particular."

"What if it wasn't about Mabel?" Rose asked.

"What do you mean?"

"Well, I happen to agree with you. I never liked the woman—and I'm sure there's plenty would say the same—but there's nobody I can think would want her dead. So what if it wasn't about her at all?"

Hugo blinked. Maybe Aunt Rose was further gone than he'd thought. "Kill Mrs Fairchild for no reason?" he asked incredulously.

Rose waved an impatient hand in the air. "Not for no reason. Nobody does anything without a *reason*, Hugo, but you and that inspector chap have both been looking for someone who wanted to kill Mabel. What if they killed Mabel to get at someone else?"

Hugo's jaw dropped.

"Doesn't it seem curious to you, that your Tommy was the last one seen with her and then she turns up dead not five minutes from his cabin, when there's not another soul in those woods for miles around?"

"I know it looks bad, but—"

"Exactly. Don't you think it looks *too* bad?"

Hugo frowned. "I'm not sure I follow what you mean, Aunt."

Rose *tsk*ed. "There can't be many people know those woods as well as the groundskeeper," she reasoned. "Don't you think if he did kill her and wanted to hide the body, he'd leave it farther than at his own front door? Those woods are big enough she might never have been found. But instead she was right on the path, where any poor fool could stumble over her."

"You're right," Hugo said slowly.

"And what's more, murderers always cover their tracks. Say something happened, he got into an argument with her or there was an accident. Wouldn't he have made sure to be seen out and about by folk in the town so there were witnesses could say he was with them?"

"So you think somebody killed her and wanted to make it look like Tommy did it?"

"It seems that way to me."

Hugo's face cracked in a broad grin. "Aunt Rose, it's *perfect!*" He leant over the bed and, in an uncharacteristic show of exuberance, kissed her on both cheeks.

"Yes, well...." She gave him a pleased smile. "I just say what I see."

Hugo was still a little dazzled by her breakthrough when he arrived home. It was such a simple twist of logic, yet one that had completely eluded him. Tommy was being made a scapegoat by the real killer, and the police were playing right into the villain's hands. All Hugo needed to do was return to the police station and speak to the inspector rather than pompous Jimmy Cooper. They could reopen the investigation and start again, find the man really responsible, the killer who had been haunting the woods only a short distance from Tommy's house.

The thought gave Hugo pause. Was it really serendipity that had placed Tommy at the victim's home shortly before her body was found beside his house, or had the murderer known Tommy was with her that day? It seemed too great a coincidence to assume otherwise, but that meant.... Hugo gulped. That meant the killer knew who Tommy was, knew where he lived, and had seen him with Mrs Fairchild on the day of her death. Which meant it must have been somebody local, or somebody watching Tommy specifically. And that person had been mere feet from Tommy's home. If Tommy had gone out earlier that morning, caught the fellow in the act.... He was a vulnerable target, out there in the woods on his own. He could have lain dead for days or even weeks before anybody bothered to look.

No. Hugo choked on the thought of it being Tommy lying on the frozen ground, Tommy with a gaping hole in his chest, Tommy's dead eyes staring sightlessly heavenward.

He gagged, trying desperately to clear the too-vivid image he had conjured of Tommy's corpse, his strong, warm flesh lying broken and blue on the forest floor. As much as he would never wish anyone dead, Hugo gave thanks in that moment that the body he had discovered hadn't been Tommy.

CHAPTER EIGHT

Hugo awoke before the alarm the following morning. He hadn't slept well, his dreams disturbed by images of Tommy lying dead in the forest or swinging from the gallows, Hugo helpless to save him. He knew what he really wanted from the groundskeeper was impossible—inconceivable—but Tommy was also his friend. Hugo thought he could be happy with Tommy's pure, innocent friendship alone.

He dressed hurriedly, forsaking his morning routine of tea and toast in order to rush to the police station the moment he could be sure it was open. He gave thanks that Jimmy wasn't on the desk when he entered the building, the front office manned instead by Constable Banks, an older chap Hugo had got to know during his time with the Home Guard. Charlie Banks was approaching retirement, a man who had never been dynamic, not even in his youth, but he was a patient soul and eminently fair. He would listen, Hugo was sure of it.

"I need to speak to the inspector," Hugo said without preamble.

"Hugo Wainwright, as I live and breathe!" Charlie rose, hand outstretched. "And what brings you here? Nothing bad, I hope."

"I need to speak to Inspector Owens," Hugo repeated, enunciating slowly.

"Is he expecting you?"

"No, but I need to speak with him. It's about Tommy Granger."

"Oh, well in that case, he'll be right out." Charlie beamed. "We're releasing Mr Granger right now."

"You—you are?" The self-righteous wind taken from Hugo's sails, he could only gawp at the constable, his mouth opening and closing without any coherent words emerging. Finally, the spell broke. "So then you know Tommy's innocent? Did you find who really did it? When will he be released? Am I allowed to see him?"

Charlie laughed. "Hold your horses, Hugo. I never said nothing about Granger being innocent. We're just choosing to let him go for now, is all."

"Hang on, what does that mean?" Hugo demanded. "You arrested him, he was charged, but now you're letting him go? Have you got any evidence against him or not?"

Charlie looked uncomfortable. "Come, Hugo, that's police business, you know it is. I can't be seen discussing the case with you, even if you are a witness."

"But I read in the paper Tommy was going to court—"

"Ah. Well." Charlie tugged the collar of his neat white shirt. "Don't know where the reporter got that from."

"You mean it wasn't true?"

"Not entirely. Oh, we'll get 'im, have no fear, but some of the details might have been a bit... hasty."

Hugo smiled grimly. He had a pretty good idea from whom the reporter had got his story. Jimmy Cooper had always been a blabbermouth.

The sound of a heavy, metallic door closing echoed from the bowels of the building, electrifying Hugo's skin. He turned expectantly to face the thick oaken door marked PRIVATE that separated the front office from the interior of the police station.

THE DEAD PAST

"Listen, Hugo." Charlie leant forward, his hand on Hugo's arm, the grip too tight to be entirely friendly. "You're a nice chap, so I'll give you fair warning. That Granger, don't let 'im get to you. He might look like butter won't melt, but he's a wrong 'un through and through. It doesn't do to get too close to the likes of 'im."

Hugo shook the man off, his distaste apparent in his expression. "Thanks for the warning, but I'll choose my own friends," he said coolly. "I think I know who to trust."

Charlie's face hardened, his flinty eyes narrowing, thin lips growing thinner. "Be like that, then. Just don't say I didn't warn you. We're letting 'im go for now, but we'll get 'im, Hugo. It's only a matter of time before a man like that slips up."

Hugo's blood ran cold at his words, but he held his retort as the interior door opened and a pale-looking Tommy emerged, Inspector Owens hard on his heels. Hugo could have laughed with relief. He struggled to refrain from crossing the room and pulling Tommy into his arms to reassure himself the man was really free. Instead, he flashed him a brilliant smile, which only grew broader at Tommy's puzzled expression.

"Tommy—thank God! Are you all right?"

Tommy swallowed and nodded uncertainly. He had dark rings around his eyes, and Hugo doubted he'd slept a wink since being arrested.

"Well, come on, I'm here to take you home. I can, can't I, Inspector?"

Inspector Owens looked from one to the other, a contemplative expression on his face. "Friends now, are we?" he asked, his tone so nonchalant, Hugo was immediately wary.

"In a way," Hugo replied carefully.

"Yet you were strangers not a fortnight ago."

"Yes. It's funny how discovering a murdered body will give a chap something to talk about," Hugo said, his tone clipped.

"Can I go or not?" Tommy demanded, cutting between them.

The inspector gave a long-suffering sigh. "For now," he conceded. "But don't think this matter is over, Mr Granger. Either of you." His cold gaze swept Hugo from head to foot. "We are continuing this investigation, and I assure you, I always get a result."

"Come on, Tommy." Hugo took his friend's arm, suffering the inspector a withering look of his own. "Let's get you home."

*****

Tommy's cabin smelt damp and musty, the cold having settled within the wood and soft fabrics after two days without a fire in the hearth. Tommy began one immediately, raking out the grey ashes and layering newspaper and dried sticks carefully over the metal grill of the stove. Lighting a match, he coaxed the kindling into flame before adding more wood, and finally, a few precious lumps of coal. Hugo watched, mesmerised by the brisk, efficient movements of Tommy's hands, the way he delicately placed each piece just so in order that it would catch and not put the fire out.

When Tommy was finally satisfied, he closed the stiff iron door with a dull clang and set about emptying and refilling his kettle in the stone sink. The tap had a pump handle, Hugo noted, and he assumed the water was drawn from an offshoot of the river below the woods. Piped water had been introduced to Puddledown some decades earlier, but clearly word hadn't yet reached this small outpost in the woods. Hugo's house, and the cottages around it, had been upgraded just before the war, and he thought gratefully of his indoor bathroom, with its gleaming pipework, remembering only too well the misery of an outhouse in snowy December.

THE DEAD PAST

Kettle on, Tommy set the tea things on the table and discarded the withered remains of the yarrow, which had dried up and died in its jar.

"It's a pity," Hugo said, crunching a shrivelled flower between his fingers. "Will you replace it?"

"Mebbe," Tommy muttered. "If I see anythin' which catches my eye."

Hugo nodded. "It's a nice touch. Brightens the place up. I never seem to have time for flowers, myself, but I do like them. Perhaps in spring—"

"What are you doing?" Tommy demanded roughly, interrupting Hugo's train of thought, which had strayed as far as bringing Tommy roses from his garden, in season. A foolish, romantic notion, and one best not given voice. "Here, I mean. What are you doing here?"

Hugo flushed crimson. "I wanted to make sure you were all right," he mumbled, rising from the table and jamming his flat cap over his sandy hair. "I realise now I'm intruding. I'm sorry—"

"I didn't say leave." Tommy's hand on Hugo's arm stilled him. "I've got the kettle on now. You might as well stay for a cup."

Hugo sat, removed his cap, and twisted it in his hands. Tommy stood, his arms folded over his chest, looking down on him. At length he sighed and sat, pinning Hugo to the spot with his dark-eyed stare.

"Why were you at the police station?" Tommy asked.

"I, I had a theory—about the real murderer."

A slow smile crossed Tommy's lips. "So you don't believe I was the one what done it?"

"Of course not!" Hugo declared staunchly.

"Go on, then." Tommy kicked back in his chair and lit a cigarette. "Let's hear this theory of yours."

Hugo dropped his cap and leant forward, putting every ounce of earnestness he possessed into his words as he explained to Tommy what Rose had suggested about him being a scapegoat for the real killer. Tommy listened in silence, his eyes growing wider and his cigarette dying forgotten in the ashtray as Hugo punctuated his speech with sharp jabs of his blunt fingers against the rough tabletop. The kettle's shrieking interrupted Tommy as he was about to answer, and he turned from the table to pour the tea, leaving Hugo to wait impatiently for a verdict.

Tommy deposited two mugs on the tabletop. Hugo reached for the nearest, waving away Tommy's apology that the milk had turned.

"So you think this murderer, he knows me?" Tommy asked at length.

Hugo immediately set down his mug, nodding as he swallowed.

"But who would do that?" Tommy demanded. "It don't make no sense. That old woman never hurt a fly, an' it's not like I've made any enemies who would want to bring this sort of trouble to my door. There ain't anyone alive I've harmed enough to want to do something like that."

"There's no one you can think of?" Hugo asked desperately. "*Think*, Tommy."

"I think I'd remember," Tommy said, a hint of steel in his voice. "I'm tellin' you, there ain't no one would do something like this."

Hugo averted his eyes, crestfallen. He'd been so *sure*....

Tommy grinned, suddenly bashful. "You really don't believe I done it, do you?"

"Of course not!" Hugo replied, shocked Tommy had to ask again.

"Why not?" Tommy asked curiously, leaning forward. "You don't know me from Adam, so what makes you so sure I'm not a murderer? Everyone else seems to believe it." The last was added with more than a touch of bitterness.

Hugo looked straight into Tommy's dark, fathomless eyes. "I just know it. I know *you*. You're not a cold-blooded killer."

"The hell I'm not!" Tommy declared angrily, shoving away from the table so forcefully their tea slopped out of their mugs, making Hugo jump. "You think I haven't killed people, Hugo Wainwright? You, with your Reserved Occupation an' books an' your cushy life—you think I'm not *capable*, but I'm telling you, I am. We all are, when it comes down to it."

"That, that's different," Hugo protested, trying not to let Tommy's words sting. "It was war, enemy soldiers—"

"They're all men," Tommy snapped. "They was only different from me because of the uniforms we wore. Regular blokes: fathers, sons, brothers, husbands.... We all mowed each other down just the same. There's no saying how many I've killed, nor any of us. You, Hugo,"—he rounded the table to lay a heavy hand on Hugo's shoulder—"yours are the only clean hands amongst us."

Hugo cringed. Tommy was right, Hugo couldn't begin to imagine what he had been through in the war, and orders or not, free choice or no, Tommy almost certainly *had* killed other men. Did the fact those men were German, or Italian, or of any other nation, mean their lives were somehow lesser, that they didn't count?

"I-I'm sorry," he said softly, not lifting his eyes from the worn, scratched surface of the table. "You're right, I don't know anything. I should have kept my mouth shut."

"I didn't mean that," Tommy said, contrite, loosening his grip on Hugo's shoulder, his touch turning soft, almost caressing. The hairs on the back of Hugo's neck prickled with awareness. "The world needs men like you, Hugo. Otherwise there'd be no good in it."

Hugo turned in his seat to look at Tommy, but the groundskeeper had moved away, his back to the table. A deep silence stretched between them as lines of tension crept through Tommy's body until at last, like a broken puppet, he seemed to sag all at once.

"Don't mind me," he said. "It's been a queer couple of days. I don't rightly know what I'm sayin'."

"It's all right," Hugo said, rising and slowly approaching him. He reached to touch him, but lost his nerve and withdrew, swallowing hard. "We're friends, aren't we? I'd like to imagine I could say anything to a friend and not have them take offence."

"Why do you want to be friends with me?" Tommy asked, facing Hugo.

"Because...." Hugo flushed anew. "You were kind to me."

"Is that all?" He seemed taken aback.

"It's no small thing, being kind to strangers," Hugo said, hoping he wasn't making himself seem more pathetic in Tommy's eyes than he already had. "You, you're a good man, Tommy Granger. I just know it. And I know you're no murderer!" he added fiercely, with every ounce of conviction he could muster.

Tommy's lips twisted and, just for a moment, the sunlight caught his eyes and they shone a fraction too brightly, their liquid darkness like infinite, glossy pools. Then the illusion was gone. Tommy blinked and looked away, a sad, wistful smile on his lips as he slowly shook his head.

"You're too nice to me, Hugo Wainwright. Too nice for your own good."

"Well, maybe." Hugo gave what he hoped was a self-effacing grin. "But you must be tired. I should let you sleep."

"I am tired," Tommy admitted, scrubbing a hand through his messy hair, making it even messier. "Couldn't seem to nod off in that damn cell."

"I understand." Hugo squeezed his arm sympathetically, then retreated. "Why don't you tell me what you need, and I'll bring it over after you've had a rest?"

"I can't let you do that!" Tommy exclaimed.

"Nonsense." Hugo waved the protest away. "You need milk, at the very least, and I doubt you want to go into town right now."

"I'll have to face them eventually," he said, but it didn't sound as though his heart was in it.

"Well, not today." Hugo dipped his head, forcing Tommy to meet his eyes. "Now, tell me, what do you need?"

Tommy shrugged helplessly. "Milk...."

"Bread?" Hugo guessed. "Meat?"

"I couldn't let you—"

"Please. I barely use my ration as it is."

"You're takin' my coupons," Tommy said with a growl, and Hugo laughed.

"All right, I'll take your coupons. Now tell me honestly, what do you need?"

Half an hour later, armed with a short list and a wicker basket, Hugo entered the town, having ordered Tommy to rest while he was gone. It felt good, doing something to help his friend, making a practical gesture for once. It felt like progress.

He took his time in the shops on Main Street, picking up a couple of sweet, sticky buns alongside the small loaf Tommy had requested, and a jar of beef dripping in addition to the pork sausages. On his way back to the cabin he passed a gorse bush still resplendent in brilliant yellow despite the recent frosts, and he wrestled with the thick and thorny branches to snap off a stem for Tommy's kitchen table.

He let himself into the cabin quietly, fearful of disturbing Tommy. He needn't have bothered. Soft snores alerted him to the groundskeeper's whereabouts, sprawled on the horsehair sofa, fast asleep. Hugo placed the wicker basket on the table and crossed the room, treading carefully lest the creaking floorboards disturb his friend.

A rush of affection rose in Hugo's chest as he looked at Tommy. He was lying full along the cushions, his legs curled to fit, his head awkwardly propped against the arm. Dark lashes fanned his cheeks, and in sleep, he seemed much younger than his twenty-seven years. Barely a man at all.

Taking the colourful patchwork blanket from the back of the sofa, Hugo gently covered Tommy and tucked him in, smiling as Tommy curled his fingers around the material in his sleep and pulled it under his chin. Hugo couldn't resist stroking a strand of hair from Tommy's forehead, but retreated a step when Tommy butted his head into his hand, unconsciously nuzzling closer, a sigh on his lips that could have been a word, a name, or merely wishful thinking on Hugo's part.

Tiptoeing back to the table, Hugo unpacked the basket and put his purchases away, arranging the gorse flowers neatly in the jar dead centre on the table. He drew the curtains against the winter sunlight streaming in from outside and left, closing the door softly, the sound of Tommy's gentle snores following him down the path towards home.

CHAPTER NINE

Hugo devoted the following day, Sunday, to the novel he'd been putting off reviewing for his editor. Even with his mind more at peace now Tommy was out of gaol, he still couldn't focus, and felt it would have been nothing short of a miracle if his finished article was even coherent at this rate. It was galling, his sudden inability to concentrate on even the most mundane task.

It might not be much, being the Arts and Literature correspondent and resident reviewer of the *Gazette*, but Hugo prided himself on always doing a thorough job. He liked to think he went the extra mile to earn his generous £500 a year salary. His mama always said he'd fallen on his feet the day he landed that job, and Hugo was inclined to agree. He didn't want to do anything that might displease his editor.

Instead of reading, however—or reading and *absorbing*, at any rate—Hugo found he was drifting, daydreaming.... Imagining a small, tousled figure lying along his sofa, snoring gently as Hugo tamped down the tobacco in his pipe and filled the room with clouds of dense, pungent smoke.

A part of him wished he'd been brave enough to stay

with Tommy on Saturday. He could have made himself useful around the cabin—quietly, of course, and only in the main room—he could have tidied, dusted, aired the place out while the cheerful fire in the little stove took the damp from the air. When Tommy awoke, Hugo could have fried up the bread and sausages in dripping, made Tommy laugh with some witty retelling of his adventure with the gorse bush, and afterwards they could have shared the sweet sticky buns, sitting side-by-side on the horsehair sofa, a real fire roaring in the hearth.

And afterwards.... Here Hugo's fantasies ground to a halt, the idyll he had painted fading into a cloud of smoky black, for Hugo didn't know what, precisely, he wanted next. One ought to go to bed after an evening by the fireside, after the flames and fumes had worked their soporific magic and made them lean lazily against one another. Would that leans turned to looks, and looks to kisses....

Hugo bit the inside of his cheek until tears pricked his eyes: an action that was becoming almost second nature, it seemed, since he had first set eyes upon Tommy. Yes, Tommy was the reason for it all: Hugo's distraction, his inability to concentrate, even his rekindled interest in life, and all the sweetness there was to be found therein.

Hugo wouldn't have it any other way.

He was wary, however, of being too forward, of forcing his company upon his newfound friend. Hugo hadn't known many folks who could honestly say they took pleasure from his company, it being more frequently tolerated than sought out, and the thought of having Tommy issue a rebuff was too terrible to contemplate. Tommy, who had first done and then said such kind things, who had looked at Hugo with compassion, and perhaps tears, in his eyes. Who had gone so far as to offer up some details from his past, shared his story, and extended a hand of friendship to the bookish, friendless man with whom Fate had thrown him together. No, to be rejected by Tommy now would be the most terrible thing of all.

So Hugo fretted and fussed, resolved to pull up his britches and pay Tommy a visit, and yet never left his house. Restless day turned to sleepless night, and Hugo found himself once more awake when the alarm sounded early Monday morning. A creature of habit, Hugo had remained in bed until the incessant ringing pierced the silence of the morning, as though to rise earlier would be to usher in the Devil himself to wreak havoc upon his neat, orderly life. He washed and dressed and read his newspaper over tea and toast and strawberry jam. Not his mama's, alas, and it never would be again, but the jars the greengrocer sold made up for what they lacked in bitter nostalgia with flavour and consistency. Once more, Hugo picked up his book, and once more he struggled and failed to comprehend a single word he was reading.

He paused for a brief luncheon of boiled ham sandwiches, and had returned to the blasted book when he was saved by a formal-sounding knock at the door. Discarding the unworthy tome in a heartbeat, Hugo, who so seldom received visitors and was always wary of those he did, all but skipped to answer the door.

Whatever happiness Hugo may have felt at the interruption was soon forgotten, however, as the door opened to reveal the grim figure of Inspector Owens, notebook in hand and an officious-looking scowl on his full moon face.

"Mr Wainwright, may I have a word?"

The inspector all but barged Hugo out of his own doorway as he spoke, by which Hugo took the question to be largely rhetorical.

"How can I help you?" Hugo asked, closing the door and trying not to let his irritation show as he followed the inspector into his front parlour and watched the man take a seat without waiting to be invited.

"I must ask for a full account of your actions since I

saw you leave the police station on Saturday morning."

"I've been here, by and large," Hugo replied, sitting in his favourite armchair, opposite the inspector. "But what's this about?"

"I will need your *precise* movements, please, Mr Wainwright. 'By and large' does not assist police investigations."

Hugo bristled. "Investigations into *what*?" he demanded.

"There has been another murder—"

"Oh, God." Hugo paled. "Please, not Tommy—"

The inspector looked surprised. "And why would you suppose Mr Granger to be the victim, Mr Wainwright?"

"Because there's a bloody lunatic out there in those woods!" Hugo snapped, barely registering the curse as it left his lips.

The inspector scratched something into his notebook with a stubby pencil.

"So.... Tommy isn't dead?"

"No, Mr Wainwright, he isn't. Although I must say, your concern for him is... *touching*." Something about the way he said the word made Hugo shiver.

"W-Who, then?" he asked, ignoring and trying to appear unaffected by the inspector's insinuation. Hugo was a criminal in neither deed nor thought. The inspector couldn't arrest him simply because he disliked who he was.

Owens consulted with his notebook. "One Archibald Bucket."

Hugo shook his head. "I don't know him."

"He was employed at the Traveller's Rest, out on the High Road."

Hugo continued to shake his head. He knew the establishment, once an old coach house, requisitioned as a children's home during the war, and now once again in private hands and put to use as a hotel for folk from the train line, but he hadn't had cause to go there since the evacuees were shipped off home, and couldn't say he was familiar with any of the staff.

"Eighteen." Inspector Owens fixed Hugo with a steely glare. "He was eighteen years old. A mere boy. His mother's inconsolable."

Hugo swallowed around the nervous lump in his throat. "I'm very sorry, of course I am, but I still don't see what this has to do with me, Inspector."

"Where were you from approximately nine o'clock Saturday morning until twelve noon today?"

"Am I a suspect?" Hugo asked. "I'd like to know on what grounds—"

"We are in the process of conducting an investigation," the inspector said stiffly. "If you have nothing to hide, you won't mind cooperating."

Hugo glowered. "I left the station and took Tommy home," he said. "I returned to town for some groceries. I'm sure if you speak to Mr Fletcher, Mrs May, or Mr Ledbetter, they'll corroborate my story."

"And what time was this?" Owens asked, scratching away at his notebook.

"I'd say I was done about twelve."

"And from there?"

"I went back to Tommy's cabin. He was asleep so I—so I left. I put the groceries away, and I left."

"And came straight home?"

"That's right."

"And you haven't been anywhere since?"

"No, I already told you. I've an article to finish for my editor—I'm a correspondent—and I've been working on that."

"You haven't had any visitors?"

"None," Hugo said.

"So you haven't seen Mr Granger since approximately one p.m. on Saturday?"

"No. But you can't possibly think Tommy had anything to do with this!" Hugo exclaimed, horrified by the implication of the inspector's words.

"You just answer my questions, Mr Wainwright, and let me do my job."

"This, this man, this Bucket—what if he knew something, about the first murder, I mean? What if he was a, a witness?"

The inspector looked up, curiosity written across his previously bland and impassive features. "A witness, you say? Interesting.... And what could he possibly have witnessed that would make him a target, when the only 'witnesses' we have on record are yourself and Mr Granger, and you're both unharmed?"

"We only found the body." Hugo shook his head impatiently. "What if this other chap saw the murder?" His analytical mind was whirling now, following the thread. "Yes, it makes perfect sense. If he worked at the Traveller's, and the murderer stayed there...."

"You think somebody went to the trouble of taking a train to Puddledown and put himself up in a hotel in order to kill Mrs Fairchild and leave her body in the woods?" The inspector's tone rose incredulously.

Put like that, it did seem rather a fanciful theory, even Hugo had to admit.

"And then, not content with committing one murder, the villain commits another two weeks later—"

"Are you sure about that?" Hugo interrupted. "I mean, was the body... was he killed recently?"

Inspector Owens grimaced. "We'll need the coroner's report to be sure. Which is why we're documenting the movement of key persons—"

"You mean suspects." Hugo's voice was flat.

"I meant exactly what I said," Owens said firmly, closing his notebook with a decisive snap and rising from his chair.

Hugo rose, too. "Is that all?" he enquired, his tone frosty.

"For now." The inspector approached the front door, pausing with his hand on the latch. "Allow me to speak frankly. I don't know how involved you are in this business, but you seem a decent sort of fellow. You don't want to get yourself mixed up with the likes of Thomas Granger."

"As you say, Inspector, you don't know." Hugo leant across the man to unlatch the door, holding it open for him. Owens hesitated for a second, an uncertain look sweeping over his face before he exited, bidding Hugo good day.

It took all of Hugo's willpower not to slam the door on the inspector's retreating back. He was shaking, he realised as he returned to the front parlour; the subtlest of tremors, but shaking nonetheless. He lit his pipe to calm his nerves, losing himself in the familiarity of routine, even though he was usually strict about only taking tobacco of an evening. It wasn't every day one was questioned by a police inspector about a murder.

There was comfort to be found in filling the bowl of his favourite briar, tamping and lighting the rich tobacco, and savouring the earthy flavour of the cool smoke. Hugo allowed himself an accompanying tot of brandy for his nerves and spent a pleasant half hour choosing quite deliberately not to think of Inspector Owens or the reason for his visit.

At the first trace of damp in the stem, Hugo extinguished the pipe with a yellowed thumb and set it in the ashtray to cool. Immediately his thoughts turned to Tommy. Hugo had no doubts as to his friend's innocence, but where was Tommy now? Where had the second body been discovered? And what would it look like if Hugo were to call on Tommy's cabin in the woods? For all he knew, the place was a crime scene for the second time in as many weeks. Hugo well remembered the hordes of police constables and officials tramping through the woodland, poking and prying and taking notes, from the day he had discovered Mrs Fairchild's body. Surely his presence would be noted and somehow twisted to damn

Tommy or himself, or both of them.

No, as hard as it was, Hugo knew he must stay away, for Tommy's sake if not his own. It wasn't like his presence was required, anyway. Hugo almost laughed aloud. What possible comfort would Tommy derive from him being there? Foolish, sentimental notion.

Hugo was self-aware enough to realise he needed to find some occupation to see out the day. Reading was less than useless. Not even his old and best-loved tomes could help him. Physical labour, that's what his present state of agitation called for. Some task that would exhaust him so thoroughly, even thinking would become impossible. Fortunately, Hugo knew of just such a chore.

Doffing his pullover and rolling up his shirtsleeves, he took the old axe from its hanger behind the kitchen door and stepped out into the chilly, late-October air. The woodpile in his garden was already stacked neatly enough, but earlier in the autumn he'd had the idea of moving it into his disused outhouse, the better to keep it safe and dry before the snow came. He much preferred a real fire to the unsightly gas contraptions, which—unlike indoor plumbing—were a modernisation he continued to resist.

Hugo was proud of his garden. The vegetable patch at the bottom had been extended during the war until only a small strip of grass ran up the centre, forming a path between two neat, rectangular beds. In the summer it would boast a full bounty of vegetables, but now, in late October, the ground was dug over and bare, the rich earth lying fallow until spring. At the end of the garden, the old coop stood, looking neglected and forlorn without any chickens. He would whitewash it next, he decided, and maybe buy a couple of hens; start over.

The wood piled next to the coop came from Tommy's forest, purchased from the overseer for a decent price, and through the long years of the war and after, it had supplemented his meagre supply of coal nicely.

Hugo was shivering as he commenced chopping and

restacking the wood, but he soon warmed up, a sheen of sweat glistening across his skin that he wiped from his forehead with the back of his hand between strokes of the axe, his sandy hair falling loose from its neatly Brylcreemed wave into his hazel eyes. The rhythm of the work was lulling, soothing, all his senses and even his busy brain completely absorbed with the task. He didn't hear anything until a voice spoke right beside him, making him leap with alarm.

"Steady on." Tommy laughed, taking hold of the axe to stop its wild trajectory as Hugo flailed his arm. "I did knock," he said apologetically. "You mustn't have heard."

"Clearly." Hugo blinked, still a little startled. "What are you doing here?"

Tommy released the axe and took a step back, his face falling. "I didn't mean to disturb—"

"Nonsense." Hugo seized his wrist to prevent him from leaving. Both men looked at the place where their skin touched, and Hugo hastily let go. "At least have a cuppa."

Tommy nodded and followed him into the kitchen via the back door.

"I must look a frightful state," Hugo muttered, whirling about his kitchen, setting the kettle on to boil and searching frantically for a cloth with which to wipe himself down. He tried surreptitiously to check the odour from his armpits, but stopped when he saw Tommy smirking.

"Didn't reckon you one for manual work," Tommy said, taking a box of matches from his pocket and lighting the gas ring under the kettle, which Hugo had failed to ensure had caught. The flame roared to life, and he took a hasty step backwards.

"I'm not," Hugo admitted ruefully, washing his hands and forearms in the sink. The front of his shirt was rumpled and stained from the wood bark, and his pullover was still in the parlour where he'd left it. He felt a veritable heathen, entertaining in shirtsleeves and suspenders.

"Seem to be doing a decent job of it," Tommy said, taking a seat at the kitchen table and politely averting his eyes as Hugo tidied up as best he could. "Putting it inside for the winter, were you?"

"That's right." Hugo willed his hands steady as he laid out mugs and milk and sugar. Hastening to the pantry, he returned with the last of Mrs May's Christmas fruitcake, which he had eked out a little at a time over the year, storing it carefully in a tin lined with wax paper. Hugo cut into it, laying two thick slices on saucers, not meeting Tommy's eye as he put his slice before him.

"Here, no, I can't take that," Tommy said immediately, pushing the plate away.

"I insist," Hugo said, brushing loose crumbs into the sink and folding the wax paper away.

"But it's your last slice."

"Then it's only right I should share it." Hugo turned, gifting Tommy with a genuine smile. "Please. I ate the rest of it on my own."

"Well, thanks." Tommy picked out a currant and popped it into his mouth, returning the smile as he savoured the unexpected treat. "An' thanks for the other things, too. On Saturday, I mean."

"Don't mention it."

The kettle whistled, and Hugo filled the teapot while he waited for a sudden blush to leave his cheeks. Why couldn't he accept a simple "thank you" without embarrassing himself?

"How did you even find the place?" Hugo asked when he finally trusted himself to speak.

"Had to ask," Tommy admitted. "I found the street right enough, from what you told me. Your neighbour at the top of the lane pointed me to the house."

Hugo nodded, wondering what old Mr Perkins in the first house on Ferndale had made of Tommy. Then he realised he didn't care and, liberated by the thought, he placed the teapot on the table and took the seat opposite his friend, letting the tea leaves infuse.

"Inspector Owens was here earlier," Hugo said.

Tommy scowled. "Thought he might be."

"Is that why you're here?"

"Had to get out," Tommy admitted, scrubbing a hand through his messy hair. Hugo longed to brush his fingers through it, lay it flat. To distract himself, he slowly swirled the contents of the teapot and commenced pouring.

"Bad up there, is it?" he asked, keeping his tone conversational.

"The young lad, they're saying, from the hotel." Tommy shrugged. "I don't know...."

"Did you find him?" Hugo asked sharply, concern knotting his insides.

Tommy shook his head. "One of the whippers-in, from the hunt. He were down that ditch we dug out."

Hugo nodded, pushing the sugar bowl towards Tommy. The man looked like he could use an extra spoonful.

"I didn't hear the hunt," he said, wondering as he did so why he'd fixed upon such an inane detail.

"No, they barely got started. Hounds must've smelt the body—" Tommy broke off, his hand flying to his mouth. "I'm sorry—"

"It's all right." Hugo touched the hand Tommy had wrapped around his mug. "It's the shock, that's all."

"Days, he must have been there," Tommy continued, as though Hugo hadn't spoken. "Lyin' in a ditch with his throat slit." He choked and struggled to compose himself.

"Brings back memories, does it?" Hugo asked gently. They hadn't discussed the worst Tommy had seen in the war, but Hugo had heard the stories of others and possessed a vivid imagination.

Tommy nodded miserably and took a long swallow of his sweet tea. "I'm not normally like this," he said with a grimace.

"At least they've found him now," Hugo said.

"An' they think I was the one what done it!" There was something desperate in Tommy's dark eyes as he looked at Hugo. "You don't believe it, do you?"

"Of course not," he replied staunchly.

Tommy nodded, reassured. "I knew you wouldn't. You're the only one what believes in me."

"It doesn't matter what people believe," Hugo said. "You're innocent, so they'll never be able to prove otherwise."

"You think innocent men never go to gaol?" Tommy asked scornfully.

"I won't let it happen," Hugo declared.

Tommy released a half-strangled laugh. "You won't be able to stop it," he said. "But thanks. It's nice to know there's someone in my corner."

"Always," Hugo replied softly, then hung his head as a blush burnt his cheeks.

"What did the inspector want?" Tommy asked after a moment.

Hugo cleared his throat. "He asked me about my movements since Saturday."

"If you'd been with me, you mean?"

Hugo nodded glumly and picked at his slice of cake. He didn't attempt to eat it.

"What did you tell him?"

"The truth. I said I hadn't seen you since Saturday."

"He weren't killed yesterday," Tommy said with conviction. "I didn't have a proper look, but I could tell that much. The huntsmen thought the same."

"Well, you were in the gaol since Thursday," Hugo said.

"He were alive Wednesday, though."

"You saw him?"

Tommy nodded miserably.

"I, I didn't realise you knew him," Hugo blustered. "He worked out of town—"

"I was at the hotel, all right?" Tommy snapped. "I only

wanted to get out of the house for a bit, go for a quiet drink. The folks in town was still talkin' about me, so I wound up there."

"He was working?" Hugo guessed, making an effort to gentle his tone.

"At first." Tommy shrugged. "We got to talkin' an' when he were done, he had a pint with me."

Jealousy pickled Hugo's gut. Irrational and unfair, but unmistakable nonetheless. "What did you talk about?"

"That ain't nobody's business but our own," Tommy growled. "Like I told the inspector, I never met the lad before. We had a couple of drinks, an' then we left."

"Together?" Hugo fought valiantly against the ugly, green-eyed thing rearing in his belly, like the dragon slain by St. George. He had no right being jealous of Tommy's friendship with anybody, and certainly not a young man who was now dead. But jealousy is never rational, and it paid Hugo's reason little heed.

Tommy scowled. "Yes, together. I bet half the folks in there saw us leave. We was goin' the same way. He went back to his house, an' I went to mine. Fell asleep an' didn't wake 'til the inspector came hammerin' on my door." He sighed softly. "He didn't deserve to die like that."

"What was he like?" Hugo asked, hoping Tommy was about to describe some grotesque deformity or foul manner in the boy.

"He was nice," Tommy said, shattering Hugo's hopes. "Seemed smart an' funny. Made me laugh, anyway. Didn't seem to mind that the other folks was givin' me a wide berth. He should have been workin' somewhere better than the Traveller's, that's for sure."

Hugo recalled what little he knew of the hotel. The Traveller's Rest was located a mile or two out of Puddledown, along the High Road towards Puddledown train station. Not many of the townsfolk ever visited the place—at least, not for any good purpose. It had once been the old coaching inn, built two centuries earlier from hard-wearing grey stone, now picturesquely weathered. The hayloft had long since been converted, first to servants' quarters, then more recently to the owners'.

Since the evacuees had left, the building had transferred into the hands of a middle-aged couple who'd moved to Puddledown from Dorchester seeking a slower way of life for their advancing years. Hugo didn't know how the place managed to stay open, given how little reason anyone would have to travel through Puddledown, but Dorchester was only half an hour away by train, and he supposed some folk preferred to stay out of the city, where rooms were cheaper. He couldn't blame Tommy for going there to get away from the gossip of the townsfolk.

"I don't think I ever met him," he said. "Was he from around here, originally?"

"Bristol," Tommy answered. "Least, from his accent. Said his pa bought it in the war an' his mam moved here for a fresh start."

"When was this?" Hugo demanded, a sudden chill seizing his heart.

Tommy shrugged. "He didn't say."

"Did he have a sister?"

"That's right, Emily. But how do you know? I thought you said you never met him?"

Hugo slumped unhappily in his chair. He'd told Inspector Owens he didn't know the victim, but he did. Archie Bucket, a slight, blond-haired boy with big blue eyes—angelic eyes—and a quiet, soulful manner, had joined the school back in '42, when he was almost twelve years old. Children had come and gone all the time in those days, and there were so many of them a schoolmaster couldn't be expected to remember them all, but still guilt crawled along Hugo's spine as more and more memories of the boy came rushing back to him. Archie, giving up his milk to the younger children; taking the little 'uns on his knee and drying teary eyes after they fell; protecting his sister from the rougher city children.

And somebody had slit that poor boy's throat and dumped his body in a woodland ditch. The full horror of it hit him like a steam train and he struggled to retain his lunch.

"Here, are you all right?" Tommy rounded the table, his hand a reassuring weight on Hugo's shoulder. "You've gone white as a sheet!"

"I-I'll be fine," Hugo said shakily.

"I take it you did know him?"

Hugo nodded. "At the school," he explained. "I taught the boy—taught both of them. And somebody killed him? It's too awful."

Tommy patted Hugo's shoulder and returned to his seat. "That it is," he agreed. "Like I said, he seemed a nice lad. Friendly. I wouldn't have wanted no harm to come to him."

"You planned to see him again?" Hugo asked.

A flicker of uncertainty crossed Tommy's face, his noncommittal "Mebbe" delivered a trifle too late to be wholly convincing.

The dragon inside Hugo growled, rearing in his breast. It was shameful to be jealous of Archie Bucket, to be hurt that Tommy hadn't come to him when he needed company. Hugo's house was far closer to the woods than the Traveller's, and Hugo would have welcomed a visitor. Why had Tommy forsaken him to drink alone in some awful bar where nobody respectable ever went? Why was Tommy being so secretive about his conversation with Archie, and why had the two men left together?

More to the point, if Tommy was innocent then why were all the people he spoke to turning up dead, and how could Hugo be sure he was really safe being seen in the company of his new friend?

CHAPTER TEN

"I don't want tea," Hugo said as the refilled kettle began to whistle. He lifted it onto a cool burner and turned off the gas. "Do you? I've got something stronger, if you prefer."

"You drink?" Tommy looked somewhere between incredulous and delighted as he smiled, wafting away the smoke from the cigarette he'd lit.

"Sometimes." Hugo gave a small smile of his own. "When the occasion calls for it."

"An' what's our occasion?" Tommy asked, lips twitching with amusement.

"Pick a reason." Hugo took two small glasses down from a shelf and placed them on the table, knocking the milk and sugar aside with a careless shove. The milk bottle wobbled perilously, but remained upright. "Finding another body, being grilled like a common criminal, being threatened by a police inspector. I've got whisky, brandy...?"

"Whisky's good," Tommy said with a nod.

Pleased, Hugo took an unopened bottle of single malt from its hiding place at the back of the pantry. "Been saving this one," he said, twisting the cork free. The sharp, peaty aroma of the amber liquid rose as he filled their glasses. "It's my favourite."

Tommy picked up his glass and swirled the whisky, watching the rich fluid cling to the sides. "Seems a shame to drink in anger," he said, taking a drag on his cigarette.

Hugo took a long sniff from his own glass, savouring the anticipation of the drink. "That it does," he agreed.

"To what shall we drink, then?"

Hugo thought for a moment before raising his glass in a toast, the only toast he could possibly have given. "To new friends."

A slow smile spread across Tommy's face, lighting his black eyes until the brown in them shone. "New friends," he repeated, clinking his glass against Hugo's, his eyes never leaving him as they drank.

The whisky was good, strong and rich, with deep, earthy notes and a hint of sweetness from maturing in oaken casks. It burnt a fiery trail down Hugo's throat and warmed the pit of his stomach. Both men made appreciative noises. Tommy kicked the opposite chair out from under the table, and Hugo sat.

Tommy grinned over the top of his glass as he took a second sip. Hugo watched him, affection swirling with the whisky in his belly, setting his nerves to tingling. He followed the movement of Tommy's arm, his slender fingers, as he casually knocked loose ash from his cigarette. The rich smoke rose in curling tendrils between them.

"I needed this," Tommy admitted, contemplating the contents of his glass.

"Oh?" Hugo asked. He hadn't thought when he offered, but he'd heard tales since the war of men using drink as a crutch, too haunted by their memories to stay sober. Cliff Fletcher, the butcher's boy, had gone that way, or so rumour had it. Hugo found he disliked the idea of Tommy being another sort of sad drunk.

"Nah." Tommy shook his head. "Don't drink much, me. Pa was always too fond of the ale, and I don't want to turn out the way he did."

"He was violent?" Hugo asked sharply.

"No, not really." Tommy shrugged. "He'd spend everythin' we had down at the Oak if Ma didn't get the money off him first. Drink himself stupid, he would. I'd see him sometimes, sittin' in his chair before the hearth—the fire gone out, mind—just sittin' there, with tears on his face. Ma said the First War changed him."

"I'm sorry." Hugo touched Tommy's hand, their fingers brushing for a moment before he retreated.

"He were only eighteen when he enlisted. Ma an' Pa, they was childhood sweethearts. They got married before he left, an' Beth—that's my sister—was born a year after he came back."

Hugo nodded. "The one who married a vicar and lives in Scarborough."

"That's right."

They shared a sad smile, the ruin of two generations of decent men standing like a ghost between them.

"War." Tommy snorted, taking a long swallow of his drink and stubbing his cigarette viciously in the ashtray. "It's just rich men playin' tin soldiers with other people's lives. You was lucky to stay out of it."

Hugo sighed. Lucky, maybe, but didn't it also make him the worst sort of lily livered coward?

Tommy rebuffed the notion the moment Hugo gave it voice. "We was all scared," he said fiercely. "Any man who says he wasn't is a damn liar, an' that's a fact, Hugo Wainwright. We all wanted out of it. If I had my time over, I'd find a way. Join the conchies, even. No way I'd go back to that." He shuddered, and Hugo's lips tightened in a sympathetic grimace.

"We had some here," he said. "Objectors—conchies—whatever you want to call them. They seemed an all right sort, really."

Tommy glowered. "Ain't they all from some strange church?"

"Quakers," Hugo supplied. "At least, our lot were.

'Friends,' they called themselves. 'Friends of the Germans,' the townsfolk used to say. For not fighting, that is."

"An' what about you, Hugo?" Tommy asked. "Did you never have a friend?"

Something about the way he said the word made Hugo wary, like he was stepping into a trap or had missed the punch line of a joke.

"I keep to myself mostly," Hugo answered carefully. "I don't do so well in company."

"Smart." Tommy nodded. "Alone's safest."

Hugo thought it an odd turn of phrase.

"Is that why you never moved?" Tommy asked. "You was born here, right?"

"Not quite. We moved here after my father died. Mama wanted a fresh start. I went to Dorchester Grammar, then university. Came home again after that."

"You never wanted to stay away? Move somewhere bigger—Bristol or London, mebbe?"

"I thought of it," Hugo admitted. "For a while, I swore I'd never return to Puddledown. But then I reckoned... I don't know." He shook his head. "It's not so bad, really. You mustn't have thought so, to wind up here."

Tommy grinned and refilled their glasses to the brim. "Don't judge nothin' by me," he said with a smirk. "I ain't such a reliable judge myself."

"I wouldn't say that," Hugo replied.

Tommy took a long swallow of his drink, hissing as the fiery liquid went down. "I thought of runnin' away," he said thickly. "I bet that don't sound so reliable, does it?"

"You can't do that!" Hugo declared, overcome with alarm. Running away would confirm Tommy's guilt in the eyes of the townsfolk, but more than that, it would mean Hugo never got to see the man again, and while such a course might be the most prudent, his innermost self abhorred the idea.

Tommy chuckled. "I won't," he promised. "Wouldn't give the bastards the satisfaction. I've done enough

THE DEAD PAST

runnin'." The last was added in an undertone, but Hugo caught it.

"You've been in trouble before?" he asked hesitantly.

Tommy sipped his whisky, his dark eyes hooded for long moments, the echo of the question hanging between them like the reverberation of music in the air.

"I could have been," he admitted at last, placing his glass on the tabletop and circling the rim with his index finger. Hugo followed the movement, the delicate ripple of sinew in Tommy's wrist, and took a gulp of his own drink. "Back in London."

"You... did something?"

Tommy laughed shortly, the sound tinged with bitterness. "You could say," he said. "I didn't murder nobody or nothin'." Seeing Hugo's expression, he hurried to explain. "I didn't steal nothin', either. Didn't hurt nobody at all, but they would have arrested me all the same. Things wasn't safe. The people I knew there, they weren't discreet. So I cut an' run while I still had the chance."

Hugo nodded, trying to be understanding. So Tommy had fallen in with a bad lot. He'd realised his mistake and escaped. That counted for a lot in Hugo's book, and he had Tommy's assurance nobody had been harmed. Probably something to do with the black market, buying and selling coupons or contraband. It wasn't any worse than what other people did, than what Tommy had been asked to do for King and country, for that matter. The capital was awash with disillusioned young men. It stood to reason there wasn't enough honest work for them all, not even with the Olympic preparations to provide employment.

"You look shocked," Tommy said at length. "Have I appalled you?"

"Not at all," Hugo replied, trying to conceal the lie. "A little surprised, perhaps."

Tommy laughed, light and gleeful. "Look at you, tryin'

to be all polite an' nice about it, when you really want to call me the scoundrel I am!" He leant closer over the table, his expression turned leering. "Or mebbe what you want is the details." He winked softly as he reclined again in his chair, and Hugo found himself inexplicably blushing to the roots of his hair, although he couldn't have said why. Again, the sensation of having missed out on the joke rose, as close to guilt and shame as made no difference.

"I... I...."

"Don't mind me." Tommy considered his near-empty glass with a rueful grimace. "It's the whisky. It's gone to my head."

"Have you eaten today?" Hugo asked sharply, a rush of concern chasing away his darker emotions.

Tommy squinted. "I had a round of toast," he said. "Or was that yesterday...?"

Hugo immediately rose and bustled to the pantry. His stomach growled, reminding him he'd had nothing since luncheon. It was now early evening. Outside the uncovered window the sky was dark, occasional lights from the neighbouring houses providing the only illumination in the encompassing blackness.

Tommy was still seated at the table when Hugo returned with the remains of Sunday's mutton joint and a tin of Coleman's mustard powder in his hands.

"Mutton sandwiches all right?" he asked, and at Tommy's absent nod, he proceeded to carve the remainder of the rich, dark meat from the bone. Hugo moved with economy and efficiency, plating the mutton and slices of thick, crusty wholemeal bread, mixing the mustard powder with a little water in a bowl, and setting the whole out with a pat of butter, and a knife and saucer each.

"Dig in," he urged, helping himself to a slice of bread, pleased when Tommy took him at his word and didn't stand on ceremony.

The groundskeeper ate as though he hadn't been fed in a week, an impossibility given Hugo had done Tommy's shopping not two days prior, but he thought guiltily of his well-stocked pantry and all the coupons he'd had that had gone to waste.

"There's more if you want it," Hugo said when the last of the crumbs had been wiped from their plates. "I've a side of bacon—"

"I couldn't," Tommy said. "That hit the spot just right." He patted his belly and lit another cigarette, smiling in what Hugo thought must be a reassuring manner. His glass was almost empty, but neither man moved to refill it.

"I'm sorry," Tommy said as he extinguished the cigarette.

"Whatever for?"

"Burstin' in here, drinkin' your drink an' eatin' your food, an' sayin' things what oughtn't to be said—"

"Nonsense," Hugo interrupted. "You've had a shock, and I should have thought, offering you whisky on an empty stomach. I don't imagine you got a chance to eat properly with the police there."

"No, that's right enough," Tommy said.

"Then if we forgive each other, there's no harm done."

Tommy smiled that slow, lazy smile of his. "You give me your best whisky, an' feed me mutton, then ask for my forgiveness?" He barked a laugh. "Hugo Wainwright, I declare, if ever I make an enemy, I want it to be you."

Their expressions softened as they contemplated each other, and it was on the tip of Hugo's tongue to say exactly what he was feeling. That he never wanted to be Tommy's enemy; he only wanted to be his best and dearest friend. Then the moment passed, Tommy looked away, fussing with his matchbox, and the small rattle of the little wooden sticks was enough to break the delicate spell.

Clearing his throat, Hugo said, "I worry about you, alone in those woods. Won't you stay here, at least until the villain is captured?"

Tommy started. "You don't mean that," he said sharply.

"Of course I do," Hugo retorted, a little stung. "It's not safe for you out there."

"If someone wanted to kill me—"

"Don't!" Hugo snapped, then instantly blushed scarlet. "I mean, don't assume you're safe. What if you saw something—"

"Like what?" Tommy asked. "Them woods is big enough, there could be a dozen murderers hidin' out there an' I wouldn't cross paths with any of them."

"Humour me," Hugo begged. "At least for tonight. It's dark anyway. You'll never find your way back."

"I could borrow a lamp," Tommy said, but he didn't sound thrilled by the prospect. To Hugo, it sounded like he wanted to be talked into staying.

"I could use the company," he said a little dolefully. "I should imagine you could, too."

Tommy inclined his head. Barely a fraction of an inch, but Hugo took heart from the gesture; the smallest admission that Tommy, too, got lonely.

"I've a spare bed," Hugo continued, pressing his advantage. "Plumbed bathroom, the bottle of whisky, and a side of bacon for breakfast."

Tommy laughed, and his whole face lit up. "That's the best offer I've had in years."

Hugo smiled. "Then you accept?"

Tommy's expression turned at once amused and reproachful. "Aye, I suppose I do. You'll have to let me return the favour one day. I've a third-hand sofa, a draughty outhouse, and all the fresh air you can eat!"

The two men chuckled, although Hugo couldn't deny Tommy's words troubled him. "You do have enough?" he asked, serious once more.

"I'm not starvin'," Tommy replied with a grimace. "An' there's game enough, when I catch it."

"His Lordship doesn't mind?"

"Nah." Tommy waved his hand dismissively. "What's a few rabbits here an' there? I don't touch his pheasants an' he's happy."

"Well, good." Hugo nodded. "I always liked rabbit pie."

"I'll bring 'em if you'll cook 'em," Tommy said. "Me, I usually just roast 'em on the fire. Easier."

"I've a vegetable plot out back," Hugo said, jerking his head in the direction of the garden. "Peas, carrots, onions, potatoes.... Everything. Come summer, I'll be overrun with it. You'll be welcome to help yourself."

"Very good of you." Tommy nodded thanks. "I should think of doin' somethin' myself, if I'm still here."

"Of course you will be!" Hugo declared, refusing to entertain an alternative.

Tommy simply smiled that slow, enigmatic smile of his.

They cleared the table and left the kitchen, Hugo insisting they'd be more comfortable in the front parlour. He walked Tommy through the house first, pointing out the bathroom and the room Tommy would be sleeping in. The bed hadn't been used since his mother passed, and Hugo felt his cheeks heat as he imagined Tommy lying beneath the counterpane, only a thin wall separating them as they slept.

"I'm in here," Hugo said, tapping but not opening the door to his room.

Tommy nodded, giving the closed door a curious glance as they moved back downstairs.

Perhaps Tommy thought it odd Hugo didn't sleep in the master room in his own house, but that had always and forever would be his mama's room, her presence burnt into the floorboards and the floral drapes, which Hugo had never seen fit to change. She had been gone almost three years, yet whenever he entered the room to air it out, he was sure he could still smell her: lilac and roses, Lily of the Valley, and the faint, sickly sweet undertones of her last illness, the stench of fever and death.

Hugo shuddered. He liked his room, which had been his since boyhood. He had grown up there, the pictures tacked on the walls through childhood and adolescence growing with him, Hornby train sets giving way to shelves of books in Greek and Latin, leather-bound volumes of Victorian poetry, and modern novels. The embossed floral wallpaper and ceiling had been painted white, their plainness somehow soothing to him. There were dark brown curtains, thick and heavy enough they'd remained even through the blackout, a sturdy dresser in a heavy, last-century design, and a threadbare square of carpet between the door and the bed. His dressing gown hung neatly on the back of the door, flannel in squares of darkest blue, his pyjamas folded under his pillow, and his slippers tucked side-by-side beneath the bed, which rose high on four stout legs of some dark wood, the head- and footboards stained to match.

The bed had come secondhand from Aunt Rose, who got it from an older couple she knew who had moved or died, or for some other reason had no more use for it. Fourteen years old at the time, Hugo had returned from school one Friday on the afternoon train and been thrilled to discover such an impressive and grown-up piece of furniture was to be his. It was in that bed Hugo had first explored his body, finally succumbing to the rumour and innuendoes of the boys at school. Afterwards, he had scrubbed the stained sheets until his hands were red and raw, terrified of his sins being discovered. Although Hugo had rarely repeated the experience since, he couldn't bear to let Tommy see the site of his shame, as though his transgressions were carved indelibly into the wood.

They settled in the parlour. Hugo refilled their glasses and brought the cleaned ashtray through, while Tommy, at his insistence, took over the laying and lighting of a fire in the hearth.

The flames crackling away, and the whisky once more flowing, Hugo found he was surprisingly at ease entertaining his new friend. He had opened the curtains to better air the smoke from the room through a small window at the top of the bay, the nets providing sufficient cover with the lights turned off, and the gathering darkness of the outside world lent the parlour a cosy, secretive atmosphere.

The more Hugo learnt about Tommy, the more he found to like about the man. He was surprisingly loquacious for somebody who had chosen to live alone, and Hugo wondered anew what had driven Tommy to such a measure, for he felt certain it was not a path he'd have chosen lightly. Not that Tommy didn't understand the work he'd been employed to do. He was a creature of nature, at ease in the woods he called his home, and as he spoke of his plans for the spring and summer months, Hugo watched him come alive, his dark eyes shining as he focused on a vision of a better future.

Mr McIver, Tommy's predecessor, had been forced to retire before the war, finally succumbing to arthritis and the burdens of old age, and the woodland had run wild during the intervening years, it being beyond the overseer's skill or capacity to do more than fell the older trees as they became dangerous, and keep the few pathways clear. Tommy spoke now of drainage, the removal of some trees and the planting of others, of completely altering the landscape to make the area more conducive to the habitation of game fowl and animals. His expression grew wistful as he spoke of summer evenings and misty mornings spent fishing with his father on the lake of the estate where his pa worked, and Hugo smiled, daydreaming of taking Tommy down to the River Crowe and creating some memories of their own.

"Yes, I like it here," Tommy concluded, settling more comfortably against the thickly padded cushions Aunt Rose had made for the sofa, a gift to Hugo's mama a year or two before the war.

It was how Hugo measured time—how they all did, these days. Before the war and after, between this war and the last, the halcyon days prior to the First. Odd, that his harmless, unassuming life should be measured by conflict, but there it was. Even Time had fallen victim to the muddy battlefields of France.

"Good," Hugo said, tipping his empty glass and debating another tot of whisky before bed. He was pleasantly squiffy, the alcohol and the warm fire conspiring to make him drowsy, the deep shadows and flickering amber light cast off by the flames relaxing him until he slumped in his chair, his limbs loose and heavy. "I like having you here," he mumbled, closing his eyes and beginning to snooze.

Tommy lit a match. Hugo heard it strike against the box and catch, filling the air with sweet, pungent smoke when it was extinguished. Cloying tendrils of cigarette smoke drifted over Hugo's face, caressing his cheek, and he made a contented sound as he moved against the rough pads of Tommy's warm, calloused fingers. But Tommy was sitting on the sofa... wasn't he?

"I swore I wouldn't do this again," Tommy said softly, his sweet, alcohol-laced breath ghosting over Hugo's face. "You're different, ain't you, Hugo? Tell me you're different."

Hugo frowned, aware something was amiss but unwilling to open his eyes and fully investigate. "Different," he repeated sleepily, focusing on the last word he'd caught. Different... different to what?

Tommy's hot breath came closer, rushing over Hugo in small gusts as he breathed hard. Hugo heard him swallow, registered he was nervous, and opened his eyes to look straight into Tommy's black and infinite gaze, before Tommy's eyelids swept shut and he kissed Hugo gently on the lips.

Hugo froze. Awake now, and feeling far more sober than he had a moment previous, he let Tommy kiss him, a part of him savouring every bit of the novel sensation—the softness of Tommy's lips, the taste of whisky and tobacco and something sweeter, that could only be

THE DEAD PAST

Tommy himself—even as part of him recoiled in horror from what was happening, what Tommy had done.

Hugo was pinned in his chair, Tommy's hands on the arms either side of him, his knees bracketed by Tommy's thighs. It would be so easy to surrender, to accept this was what he had wanted all along. Let Tommy kiss him, straddle him, climb into his lap and... and....

And bring them both to ruin when the full might and wrath of the law crashed down upon their heads.

The shame was more than Hugo could stand: the shame of his neighbours knowing, Aunt Rose, the memory of his sainted mama; and the shame of wanting it, of responding, not with revulsion, but with desire.

With a jerk, Hugo wrenched his head away, staring in horror as Tommy recoiled, his dark eyes liquid in the low light.

"What was that?" Hugo hissed, outrage coming easiest from the maelstrom of emotions swirling inside him.

"I thought—I'm sorry, oh God, I'm sorry!" Tommy reached for him, but halted as Hugo shrank away. "Hugo, please, I don't know what came over me. Please, let's just forget about it—"

"No." Hugo choked the word out, and Tommy grew white as a sheet, waiting fearfully for judgment to be passed. "That is, I mean, there's no harm done." Hugo tried valiantly to pull himself back together, but he felt like he'd been shattered into a thousand different pieces.

"Please," Tommy whispered. "I thought...."

"It doesn't matter what you thought," Hugo grumbled. "It's best we forget about it—both of us. We've had too much to drink."

Tommy nodded. "It won't ever happen again," he promised, and Hugo chose to ignore the way his heart sank at those words.

"Least said, soonest mended." He held out his hand for silence as he rose unsteadily from his chair. What he wanted—what Tommy had offered—was utterly and completely beyond the pale. Best not to even consider the possibility, the smallest fragment of hope.... *No!* Hugo crushed it viciously, fighting a private war with himself even as Tommy watched, anxiously fidgeting, his weight shifting on his feet until Hugo was positively seasick from looking at him.

They gave each other a wide berth as Hugo checked the guard was securely across the dying embers of the fire, closed the window, and drew the curtains fast against the cold night.

"Best go to sleep," Hugo muttered, pausing in the doorway to look back at Tommy, coloured in red and black by the firelight, his dark eyes shining and his sinful lips parted to form words that never came. "Things'll look better in the morning."

Tommy closed his mouth, his lips twisting in a grimace as he straightened, hands behind his back and legs together. "As you say," he said coolly, and Hugo almost expected a salute and click of his heels to accompany the dismissal.

With a heavy heart, Hugo mounted the stairs for his lonely bed, wondering if he hadn't just made the biggest mistake of his life.

CHAPTER ELEVEN

Hugo hardly slept that night, tossing and turning in his bed, his mind racing, reliving the brief kiss over and over. He had lain still and ashamed as the treads creaked when Tommy finally mounted the stairs, a good hour or more after Hugo had retired. He held his breath when the footsteps paused outside his bedroom door, biting the inside of his cheek until he tasted blood in an effort to remain silent, to stop from crying out for Tommy to enter and do as he pleased.

That must have been the nature of the crime Tommy spoke of earlier, Hugo realised as he heard the footsteps recede along the corridor, the door to his mama's room closing with reverberating finality. A victimless crime indeed, but a crime nonetheless, and Hugo had never received so much as a clip around the ear from a policeman in his life. To knowingly break the law, to court public disgrace.... It was unthinkable.

And yet, as the long, dark hours of night crept by, Hugo couldn't help but think of it, half-formed images playing over and over in his mind, whispers of Greek and Latin, the bawdy jokes of the fellows at university....

When his alarm finally sounded, Hugo felt as though

he hadn't slept a wink.

Hearing movement in the next room, he rose immediately, fearful of Tommy leaving, never to return. Hugo suspected he had offended his friend and, coward though he may be, he still held out hope Tommy saw something in him worthy of his friendship.

The lavatory chain rattled in the bathroom, and Hugo hastened to dress. Tommy's heavy step sounded on the stairs, and Hugo rushed to the landing, his pullover half-on and half-off, alarmed that Tommy was leaving.

"Wait up!" he called to the tousled brown head below him. "Please, don't leave yet."

Tommy looked up, a smile on his face. "I was thinking of puttin' the kettle on," he said. "Thought you might be in need of a cuppa."

Hugo returned the smile. "That sounds lovely," he said, with all the sincerity he could muster.

"Righto. Take yer time." Tommy tripped down the last few stairs, and Hugo didn't think it was entirely his imagination that the groundskeeper's step was lighter.

Feeling rather lighter himself, Hugo washed up and descended to find Tommy in the kitchen, making himself at home. Hugo paused in the doorway, watching as his friend opened drawers and searched shelves for the tea things, the kettle already on the gas burner, the dishes Hugo had left on the drainer neatly tidied away. Would this be what it was like, he wondered, if Tommy lived with him always? Rising to cheerful words and a companion with whom to share the chores and meals and long evening hours?

It was a heady romance, but a romance nonetheless. The reality, Hugo knew, would be very different. The excuses they'd have to make to curious neighbours and gossipy churchwomen, the pretence of sleeping in separate rooms, the ever-present fear of being overseen or overheard, the public disgrace that would follow discovery.... No. Hugo swallowed hard, gritting his teeth.

Better to remain alone. Alone was, as Tommy had so rightly said, safest.

"There you are." Tommy smiled as he turned and saw Hugo in the doorway. "Kettle's almost boiled."

"I'll get the bacon," Hugo said.

"There's no need—"

"I promised. I insist."

Tommy grinned. "Well, you've twisted my arm, then. I won't say no to a bit o' bacon."

Hugo nodded and proceeded to perform an awkward do-si-do around Tommy in the narrow kitchen, afraid if they touched, all his good intentions would unravel.

The kettle whistled, and Hugo jumped in alarm. Tommy's hand barely brushed his wrist, but the gesture soothed him in an instant, his skin retaining the memory of the touch as sand retains water. He was absorbing Tommy, piece by piece, hoarding memories that would keep him warm at night when he was but a sad old man, consumed with regret for what might have been.

Tommy filled the teapot and sat at the table, smoking a cigarette and sipping his brew in silence as Hugo fried up two thick slices from the side of bacon, and toasted four rounds of bread.

"You got a letter." Tommy pushed a sheet of folded paper towards Hugo as he placed their food on the table and sat. "Saw it on the doormat, reckoned you might have missed it."

Hugo took the paper, frowning. It hadn't been there the previous day when the inspector called, of that he was certain; it was too early for the postman and besides, the paper was unmarked. A note from one of the neighbours, perhaps? Cold dread seized him as he recalled the open curtains in the front parlour. What if somebody had seen them, reported them to the police, or was trying to blackmail him? He gripped the innocuous-looking paper in shaking hands, unwilling to open it and reveal his fate.

"Are you all right?" Tommy asked, looking at Hugo

with undisguised concern. "You look like you've seen a ghost!"

"Fine." Hugo cleared his throat. "I'm, I'm fine." He unfolded the paper before he lost his nerve and frowned at the message it contained.

"What is it?" Tommy asked, doing nothing to hide his curiosity.

"I, I don't know," Hugo admitted. "It means nothing to me." He lay the paper down, the name WILLIAM DAVIES in bold block capitals the only writing on the page.

"Oh God." Tommy dropped his knife with a clatter.

"What?" Hugo demanded, half-rising in his chair, looking instinctively towards the window, expecting to see a posse of police constables coming to break down his door and drag them both off in chains.

"Bill Davies," Tommy said, his face as white as a sheet. "Oh God, oh God...."

"You know who this is?" Hugo asked, picking up the paper and holding it towards Tommy. The groundskeeper recoiled, the legs of his chair scraping loudly across the tiled floor.

"It can't be," Tommy muttered, the whites of his eyes showing. "No one knew—no one! Bill Davies is dead!"

"Oh." Hugo placed the paper back on the table, settling once more in his seat. It stood to reason an attractive man like Tommy would have had lovers in the past. Tommy was brave, fearless—it had been Hugo running like a coward last night. He had no right being jealous.

"It's not possible," Tommy said, his tone muted like he was talking to himself. "No one knew. No one knew...."

"Tommy, it's all right." Hugo covered Tommy's hand with his own. "William Davies, was he, I mean, were you...?"

Tommy's eyes widened still further. "No!" he snapped, recoiling from Hugo's touch. "No, nothin' like that. We was friends, that's all."

Hugo didn't think it seemly to gloat over a dead man, but a certain sense of smugness took up residence in his mean little heart at Tommy's insistence he and William Davies hadn't been lovers.

"You wanted more?" he guessed, trying to sound sympathetic.

Tommy levelled him with a cold, flat look. "Bill was my friend," he said stiffly. "We was in the regiment together."

"Of course." Hugo blushed, berating himself for attempting to understand Tommy's wartime experiences.

"He bought it at Dunkirk," Tommy continued in a monotone, devoid of emotion. "I held him in my arms as he died. I ain't never cried so much over anyone as I did Bill Davies, an' that's the truth."

"I-I'm sorry," Hugo stammered. Pathetic, inadequate utterance, but that suited Hugo just fine. Pathetic and inadequate was what he was.

Tommy shook his head. "Not as sorry as I am."

"But why would someone put his name through my door?" Hugo wondered aloud. "It seems a pretty poor sort of message—"

"Someone *knows*," Tommy interrupted. "Someone— God, someone's been watchin' me. They must've known I was here." His pale face grew paler still as he looked at Hugo. "I've got to go. I'm puttin' you in danger. I'm sorry, I'm sorry for all of it."

"Now hold on." Hugo rose from the table as Tommy stood to leave. "What do you mean, you're putting me in danger? Who's been watching you, and why?"

"I don't know!" Tommy cried, desperation seeping into his voice. "Don't you see, someone knows what I've done. It's not safe to stay here."

"Well, you're certainly not going home," Hugo declared. "Not if it isn't safe. If this note is some sort of threat, why, we'll take it to the police station. Tell Inspector Owens what's been going on."

"You can't do that!" Tommy rounded the table and clung to Hugo, dark eyes wide and beseeching. "Please, just leave it. Let me sort it out."

"Not until you tell me what's going on."

"I don't know," Tommy said miserably. "I thought no one knew, but...." He broke off, regarding the cryptic note as though it were his death sentence.

"Knew what?" Hugo asked, gentling his tone. "Tommy, it can't be as bad as all that. Tell me, and perhaps I can help."

"There ain't no one who can help me," Tommy said sadly. "Not for what I done."

Hugo made an exasperated sound. "Try me," he challenged. "Whatever it is. Why are you so afraid of a dead man's name?"

"Because I killed him!"

Both men recoiled, staring at each other with wild eyes.

"You, you did what?" Hugo asked, sure he must have misheard.

"I killed him, all right? I am a murderer, like everybody thinks."

"Tommy... no. It, it was war. Men died all the time. I know he was your friend, but it wasn't your fault."

"Wasn't it?" Tommy sneered. "Was you there, Hugo? Did you see it happen?"

"No," Hugo admitted.

"Next you'll tell me it was someone else's hand over his mouth, someone else pinchin' his nose an' watching the light leave his eyes. Is that what happened, Hugo? Was it someone else what suffocated him?"

Hugo's head swam, and he leant a hand on the table to steady himself, Tommy's words hitting him like physical blows. Could his friend really have done such a terrible thing?

"No, I thought not." Tommy barged Hugo out of the way, making for the door.

"Why?" Hugo demanded, seizing Tommy's arm and

refusing to let go. "Why did you do it?"

Tommy's eyes were too bright when he faced Hugo. "You don't know what it was like," he said. "It were chaos. Men everywhere, nobody knowin' what was goin' on. We thought the Germans would be on us any minute...."

"What happened?" Hugo asked firmly, trying to keep Tommy calm. The man looked on the brink of a nervous collapse.

"He was hit," Tommy said sadly. "Durin' the retreat. There was blood comin' out of his mouth, all pink an' frothy. I knew it was his lungs. I'd seen others go the same way. White as a ghost, Bill was, but awake. He was awake the whole time." He wiped his mouth with the back of a trembling hand. "I couldn't leave him there to die, and I couldn't take him with me. I didn't think I had a choice."

"Oh, Tommy." Hugo tightened his grip on his friend's arm, his heart aching for the terrible burden he carried.

"So I told him he was the best friend a poor beggar like me could ever hope to have, an' I done it before I lost my nerve. I covered his mouth an' nose an' waited for him to die. Took forever, it seemed like, an' he looked at me the whole time. Looked at me like he never even knew who I was."

"I'm sorry." Hugo pulled Tommy into his arms and held him, no longer concerned who saw, or what they might make of what they were seeing. His friend was in pain, and Hugo wanted to offer whatever poor comfort he could.

Tommy clung back, clawing his fingers into Hugo's shoulders, his face buried in the crook of Hugo's neck. His breath was ragged, and he trembled like a leaf, but Hugo thought Tommy's eyes were dry. Perhaps he'd shed all his tears for Bill Davies already and had none to spare for himself now the deed was done.

"You're too good to me, Hugo Wainwright," Tommy said with a sniff, retreating from their embrace.

"Nonsense," Hugo blustered. "You did what you

thought best at the time. Nobody could ask for more."

"I killed my best friend!" Tommy cried. "An' the Germans didn't come, and we all got out! He might have lived."

"And he might have died a slow, agonising death," Hugo countered.

He couldn't deny he was shocked by Tommy's admission, but not having been there himself, he felt it improper to judge the actions of a soldier on a battlefield. It was beyond credulity to think Tommy's pitiful tale hadn't been repeated a hundred different ways on both sides of the conflict. If men shot lame horses and mad dogs to put them out of their misery, it stood to reason soldiers would put down their injured comrades just the same. Sometimes death was the kindest release of all.

"You don't have to be nice to me," Tommy said. "I know I don't deserve it."

Hugo took a deep breath. "What you did was brave," he said solemnly. "You eased your friend's suffering. There's not many folk who have it in them to do that." He paused, looking at the ceiling above Tommy's head, a direct line to his mother's room, the room in which she'd died. "My mama.... She had the fever. Miserable, it was. The doctor couldn't do anything, and I watched her—for days, I watched her—coughing and sweating and shaking, not knowing who she was half the time, thinking my father was here the other half. At night she would cry—" He shook off the memory, still too painful to revisit. How he would lie in bed, holding his pillows over his ears to block out the sound of her thin, wailing cries. "If I'd been a braver man, like you, I'd have done something. I'd have made it stop."

Tommy gave him a sceptical look. "You don't mean that," he said roughly.

"Sometimes I do." Hugo touched the back of Tommy's hand. "Everyone thinks those thoughts, watching someone they love suffer. I think it takes the very best of us to do something about them."

Tommy shuddered. "You can dress it up with your fancy words all you like, Hugo Wainwright. The fact is, I'm a murderer. Bill's blood is on my hands, an' now somebody knows what I've done."

"Who?" Hugo asked. "Someone from your regiment?"

Tommy shook his head. "I don't know."

"*Think*, Tommy." Hugo resisted the urge to grab him by the shoulders and shake. "Don't you see, this is the fellow the police are looking for. If we can only name him...."

"What?" Tommy sneered as Hugo faltered. "We can go to Inspector Owens an' tell him what I've done, an' he'll let me go? Not on your life. He'll clap me in chains an' I'll swing for sure."

Hugo paled. "Don't say that," he snapped.

"It's the truth." Tommy shrugged. "I'm a murderer. P'raps I deserve to swing."

"And what about the fellow out there?" Hugo demanded, gesturing wildly towards the window. "You think he should get away scot-free, do you? He's killed two innocent people, Tommy. That's far worse than anything you did."

"You talk like there's degrees of killin'," Tommy said sulkily. "Face it, Hugo, there's three people dead who oughtn't to be, because of me. I deserve to get what's comin' to me."

"Then whoever left this note deserves it more," Hugo said.

Tommy turned and slumped in his chair, collapsing like a broken, discarded doll. Hugo immediately went to him, sitting opposite and taking his hand.

"This isn't your fault," Hugo said softly, as Tommy made a low, keening sound in the back of his throat. "Tommy, listen to me. This isn't your fault."

"Of course it is." Tommy glared at him, his black eyes flashing dark and malevolent. He pulled away with a jerk.

"What do you know about any of it?" he hissed. "It's all right for you, Hugo Wainwright. You got to stay here teachin' schoolchildren their ABCs while we was off fightin' and dyin' in France. You don't know nothin' about it. Walking for mile after mile through mud up to yer knees, boots fallin' apart on your feet, dead men an' horses lyin' at the side of the road, rats an' flies all over them. You didn't see the towns like this one, bombed flat, children hidin' in the rubble, their clothes in rags, starvin' an' terrified. An' we was starvin', too. We'd go days without a proper meal or sleep, weevils in the biscuits, rats everywhere. The Hun hard on our heels, shells fallin', Stukas over our heads. An' at the beach, ships sunk standin' half out of the water, men makin' a swim for it, or who had tried, their bodies all swollen an' washing up all over...." He shook with the memories. "I carried Bill as best I could, but once we was on the beach, an' I saw how bad things were...."

"You gave up hope," Hugo finished for him, moved almost to tears by Tommy's words.

"I didn't have no right," Tommy growled. "Bill, he saved me more than once. I'd have been dead long before if it weren't for him."

Hugo's blood ran cold at the thought of Tommy lying broken and bloodied on a battlefield.

But Tommy was paying no attention to Hugo. He had quietened, all the anger drained from him as he turned reflective. "Bill knew what I was, an' he was my friend anyway."

"What, what you are?" Hugo asked hesitantly. "You mean—"

"Queer." Tommy's voice was flat. "A bugger, a pansy, whatever you want to call it. He could have had me reported a dozen times, but he never."

Bitter bile rose in Hugo's gorge. "You mean there were... others?"

Tommy laughed shortly. "I dunno what they was," he

said. "They just knew I wouldn't put up a fight." He looked at Hugo, his expression inscrutable. "There were tarts in the towns, would go with anyone for a couple of coins. Dirty, they were, riddled with diseases. Some of the men wouldn't touch them. Had wives or sweethearts to think of back home, didn't want to take somethin' back that they oughtn't."

"So they found you," Hugo said flatly.

Tommy nodded, his misery evident.

"You could have said no!" Hugo protested. "Reported them, or—"

"We could have been dead the next day!" Tommy snapped. "Didn't seem much point in sayin' no. An' besides, the Corp. knew what was going on. Said we was all desperate men an' turned a blind eye to anythin' he oughtn't see."

Hugo's stomach rolled at the thought of a string of nameless, faceless men using Tommy's body to slake their lusts. Of Tommy allowing himself to be used.

"I see them, sometimes," Tommy whispered. "In my dreams. Hear them gruntin', smell the stench of their sweat." He shuddered. "I don't rightly think I'll ever be clean of what they did to me. If I had my time over—but mebbe I'd do it all the same. All 'cept Bill. He didn't deserve what I done to him. Me, I deserved everythin' I got."

"You didn't deserve any of it!" Hugo declared. "None of you did."

"You was right, turnin' me down," Tommy said sadly. "I don't deserve you, Hugo Wainwright. You're too good for the likes of me. If you want to report me, tell the inspector what I done, I won't mind. You'd only be doin' what's right. An' if you don't, I'll never trouble you again, I swear it."

"You do trouble me," Hugo admitted. "You trouble me more than I can possibly say."

"I'll leave." Tommy rose once more, but Hugo was

faster, rounding the table and taking hold of his shoulders.

"Last night...." Hugo's eyes locked on Tommy's lips. "I didn't want you to stop."

Tommy looked at him, his expression wary. "What are you sayin'?" he asked hoarsely.

"I'm saying I don't care," Hugo said. "I thought I did, I thought I could be your friend and be content with that. I thought you'd never need to know how I really feel, all the terrible things I want. And maybe I should be shocked by what you've told me, but I'm not, Tommy. I'm not. I, well, if anything, I'm jealous. And angry. Angry at those men for doing that to you, but I'm also angry that they got to know you in a way I haven't, and I don't want you to leave, Tommy. I want you to stay and see if we can't get to know each other a little better, too."

"It wasn't only them," Tommy blurted. "In London—"

"I don't care," Hugo said firmly. "I only care that you're here now, and I'm here. Whatever was done to you in the past, I'll help you forget it, if you'll let me."

"You wouldn't want me," Tommy said sadly. "Why would you want me? I'm broken, Hugo. I've done some awful things, things you should rightly hate me for, as would any decent man. I weren't in my right mind last night, or I'd have never—"

Tommy released a muffled exclamation as Hugo pushed him against the wall and kissed him.

Hugo kept his eyes closed, not wanting to see alarm or revulsion on Tommy's face, wanting only to feel the softness of his lips, the sharp scrape of his beard stubble. Tommy's mouth was immobile beneath his, but Hugo held him close, their lips pressed hard together until Tommy relented, not slowly, but all at once, his body growing boneless as he leant against the wall and relaxed in Hugo's arms. Tommy opened his mouth, and the kiss deepened until Hugo tasted toast and bacon, tea and cigarette smoke. Then Tommy's tongue was at Hugo's lips, soft and slick and surprisingly cool, the most foreign sensation Hugo had ever experienced.

He jerked back with a start, shocked at the sensuality of the act. Remorse flooded to fill the distance between them as Hugo realised he was no better than the army curs who had forced their unwanted attentions upon Tommy and left him feeling he had no right to command his own body.

"I-I'm sorry," Hugo stammered, backing away. "I should never—I didn't mean to make you—"

"You didn't make me do nothin' I didn't want," Tommy said, with a hint of a smirk. "Not unless you didn't want it?"

As much as Hugo wanted to run and hide from the shameful truth—a truth he had never before dared to give voice—he recognised now was the time to be honest if ever he wanted to be so. "I, I wanted it," he said, his voice coming out husky with the effort of forcing the words through his teeth. "I've wanted to kiss you since almost the first moment we met."

Tommy pushed away from the wall and approached Hugo, his movements loose and languid, like a predator closing in on its prey. Dressed in yesterday's corduroys and shirt—not rumpled enough to have been slept in, Hugo realised with a shock—frayed black braces looped over his shoulders, Tommy was leaner and more compact than his bulky wax overcoat would have people believe. His shirtsleeves were loose, revealing delicate wrists, the milk-white V at the base of his neck indecently exposed. Hugo swallowed hard as Tommy stopped before him, so close the same breath shivered between them.

"Have you ever kissed a man before, Hugo?" Tommy asked softly, his attention focused on Hugo's lips.

Hugo shook his head.

Tommy raised an eyebrow. "Not ever?" he asked, slightly incredulously. "No boy at school, some lad at university—nobody your whole life?"

Hugo blushed for shame as he answered in the negative. Although younger than he, Tommy was an experienced man of the world. What could he possibly want with a cowardly, bookish virgin, not even brave enough to speak his desires aloud to himself?

"I wish I were like you," Tommy said, startling Hugo out of his miserable thoughts. "If I'd had you, if we'd found one another sooner...." He brushed the side of Hugo's jaw with the back of his hand, his touch so light, Hugo barely felt it. "I'd have been all right with you, Hugo. You'd have kept me right."

"I still could," Hugo said hopefully, swallowing past the lump in his throat.

"An' you really want me?" Tommy's liquid black eyes pinned Hugo to the spot, demanding nothing less than the full and frank truth.

Hugo nodded vigorously. "I do."

Tommy's lips twisted, somewhere between a grin and a grimace. "Then God help us both," he said, before sliding his hand around the back of Hugo's neck, pulling him close, and kissing him as though their lives depended on it.

CHAPTER TWELVE

It felt to Hugo as though an eternity passed before they reluctantly released each other and stepped back. Tommy's eyes were bright, his lips parted to release shallow, panting breaths, and judging by the way Hugo's pulse pounded in his veins, he looked similarly dishevelled. They grinned, then laughed, releasing some of the tension crackling between them, the laughter fading into soft, affectionate smiles, this new development in their friendship cemented when Tommy took Hugo once more into his arms and placed a last light kiss on his lips.

Hugo wanted nothing more than to block the windows, throw up the old blackouts, and shut the rest of the world outside. Hold Tommy close and kiss him over and over until day turned to night and all the seasons melted into one eternal moment in which he and Tommy were together, with not another care in the world.

The ugly note on the kitchen table, lying twisted amid the detritus of their abandoned breakfast, refused, however, to be forgotten. Reluctantly, Hugo took it up.

"What do we do now?" he asked.

Tommy shied from the paper as though it were an adder that might strike at any moment. "There ain't nothin' we can do," he said warily.

"We can't go to the police, granted," Hugo said. "I doubt Inspector Owens would take us seriously, anyway."

"What are you thinkin'?" Tommy asked, sitting at the table and lighting a cigarette.

"You're not going back to that cabin," Hugo said in a tone that brooked no refusal. "Not now we know it is you he's after."

Tommy merely raised his eyebrows and took a long drag of his cigarette. Hugo began clearing the table, emptying their mugs into the sink and rinsing them under the tap, staring out of the window at the fence separating his property from his neighbour's. It was high enough Hugo's kitchen wasn't directly overlooked, but still, he realised unhappily what a risk they had just taken.

"He must have been watching," Hugo realised. "Last night, I mean. He knew you were here."

"All the more reason for me to go," Tommy said, a hint of steel in his voice. "Two people have already died because of me. I ain't putting you in danger, too."

"He's already seen us together," Hugo pointed out. "If he was looking through the window, there's no telling what he saw."

They both paused at that. If the fellow following Tommy wanted to see him disgraced, he need only report them to the police. Hugo hoped, however, that the villain had gone too far to think of approaching the inspector for any reason. No, he was sure the man hunting Tommy was working to his own agenda.

Hugo cleared his throat. "What I'm saying is, neither of us are safe if we separate. There's no saying he wouldn't go after you if he had a chance, no matter he hasn't done so yet. For all we know, Mrs Fairchild and Archie were unlucky enough to walk through the woods and stumble across him. Maybe he's been after you all along. And even if he hasn't, if he wants to hurt you, well, I'm the only other person he'll have seen you with. That makes me a target as much as you."

Tommy started in his chair, but Hugo held out a hand to still him. The moment the realisation had struck, he'd been filled with a strange sense of calm. He should be frightened, having a murderer on his tail, but if anything, he felt exhilarated. He had kissed Tommy! After that, he could do anything.

"The way I see it, we're better off sticking together, and we'll be safer here than out in the woods," Hugo concluded.

"Until when?" Tommy demanded. "I've got my job to think of, an' your reputation. What will folk say? What reason would we give?"

"I don't care," Hugo said.

Tommy snorted. "You'd care if they came after us."

Hugo's confidence wavered. He would care if he was arrested, of course he would. He didn't want to go to gaol, to be branded a bugger, be spat at in the street. He knew what happened to men like him if they were ever found out. He looked at Tommy and his gut lurched. He didn't want Tommy to be arrested either, but neither did he want him to get hurt.

"I'll put the blackouts up," he decided. "At night, that is. The neighbours think I'm mad, anyway. At least then no one will know you're sleeping here. You can be gone in the morning before any of them are up. Nobody need ever find out."

"Mebbe, but I'll still be out in the woods during the day, an' you'll still be on your own here. If it ain't safe, then it ain't safe, whatever time we come an' go."

Hugo frowned as he put the freshly filled kettle back on the hob and lit the burner. "Then we need to find him," he said. "March the villain to the police station ourselves if we have to. They'll only have a murderer's word for what happened to Bill. They won't be able to charge you with anything."

"Mebbe I should turn myself in," Tommy countered.

"What?" Hugo set their mugs on the table with a bang.

"That's what he wants, isn't it? If I turn myself in, you won't be in danger no more."

Hugo made an impatient noise as he sat. "Don't worry about me. I want to see this fellow pay for what he's done. An old woman and a young lad are both dead because of him. Don't you think their families deserve to know what happened to them, and why?"

"How would we even go about finding him?" Tommy asked.

"Puddledown's too small to hold a stranger forever. He must be staying somewhere nearby, otherwise he wouldn't have been able to follow you yesterday. And I doubt he's the sort of chap who happens to have a pen and paper in his pocket to push messages through doors at a moment's notice. No, he watched you arrive here, and when he was sure you were staying, he left and came back with that note. Which means"—Hugo warmed to his theory—"he must want you to know what this is all about. He's punishing you."

"That's all well an' good," Tommy grumbled. "It don't help us find him."

"There's only so many places he could be staying," Hugo reasoned. "Boarding with somebody in town, perhaps. Or maybe he found an abandoned house or shed farther out. There's no telling what sort of place a desperate man might find, and there's enough farms and outbuildings hereabouts."

"An' you want us to search them all, is that it?" Tommy scowled. "It ain't possible."

"What other solution is there?" Hugo demanded.

"We could leave," Tommy said quietly. "Or I could. It ain't right, me involvin' you in this. I could go somewhere else—"

"And what if he follows you?"

Tommy shrugged. "Then at least he ain't here no more."

"No." Hugo shook his head. "No, I won't allow it. He's not driving you away, not when you're happy here."

"It's not like I ain't never moved before," Tommy said in a small voice.

"I haven't."

Tommy looked up sharply. "What?"

"You think I'm going to—blast!" Hugo rose as the kettle began to shriek and removed it from the hob, slopping boiling water over his hand as he dumped it carelessly on the countertop. Hissing under his breath, he hurried to the sink, turning the cold tap on full over his reddened fingers.

Tommy was at his side in a trice, taking Hugo's hand and gently turning it to examine the livid mark. "Just a scald," he said. "Cold water ought to help."

"I know," Hugo said through gritted teeth, his fingers throbbing as the icy water poured over them. "I'm a clumsy fool—"

Tommy smiled and stood a little closer, leaning his forehead against Hugo's cheek. "An' here you want to go playin' detective, capturing a murderer." He chuckled throatily, sending a shiver down Hugo's spine. "You can't even pour a kettle without doin' yourself an injury."

"I meant what I said," Hugo repeated, turning his hand so Tommy's fingers rubbed over his palm. "I don't want you to leave."

"An' I don't want to go," Tommy admitted. "I think I finally found a place I can be happy, an'... an' I like you, Hugo. You're not like any man I ever met before."

"I could say the same about you," Hugo said with a smile.

"Good," Tommy growled, his fingers tightening possessively around Hugo's wrist.

Tommy retreated as Hugo removed his hand from the stream of cold water and examined his fingers. "Not so bad," was his final assessment, and he filled the teapot and returned to the table to continue their conversation.

"We need to go into town," Hugo decided.

"What for?"

"You're not going back to that cabin—not tonight, at any rate—so we'll need something for supper, and any odds and ends you might need."

"I haven't got my coupons," Tommy protested.

"I've got mine," Hugo said easily.

"But won't folk talk, if they see us visitin' the shops together?"

"True." Hugo frowned. It was a Tuesday, the day after the deliveries arrived, so Main Street was likely to be busier than usual. "We'll split up," he said. "I'll go to the butcher's, and you can go to the bakery and greengrocer's. I'll give you the money—"

"I've got my own money," Tommy snapped, and Hugo blushed.

"Yes, of course. I wasn't implying—"

"Whatever you buy, we'll split the cost."

"Of course." Hugo nodded vigorously. "I didn't mean you to think—"

"It's all right." Tommy backed down. "Mebbe I was bein' sensitive. You an' me, we're different, but just because you speak in a plummy voice, that don't mean you have to pay my way."

"Of course not!" Hugo was affronted Tommy had even suggested that's how he saw their friendship progressing. Then a thought occurred to him, and his blood grew cold. It was on the tip of Hugo's tongue to ask if Tommy had ever had a friend who paid his way, but a wash of shame for even thinking such a thing held him back. He had no right to ask such a question, and whatever the answer, it wouldn't do him any good to know. That there had been other men before him in Tommy's life was enough. His only consolation was that they were all in the past, whereas he was Tommy's present and, hopefully, his future.

They buttoned up in warm coats before stepping out

THE DEAD PAST

into the cold. The early morning frost had burnt off under a sickly winter sun, but the north wind was bitter and bitingly cold. Hugo turned up the collar of his overcoat then thrust his hands deep into his pockets as they began the half-mile walk to Main Street, Tommy keeping step beside him, his chin tucked into the front of his wax jacket.

They passed a number of folk out and about in the streets between Ferndale and the centre of Puddledown, their curious glances and overly polite hellos raising the hairs on the back of Hugo's neck. What if they gossiped, what if they suspected, what if there was something in his gait or expression that gave him away?

At his side, Tommy seemed unconcerned, shooting Hugo secretive little smiles whenever somebody passed them by, like they were in on a joke that nobody else understood.

Nobody else *would* understand, Hugo thought miserably, conscious every time he glanced at Tommy that his desires were written plainly across his face. Hugo realised, with a sinking heart, that their future—should they have one—would always be like this: walking two paces apart, schooling their expressions, and hiding the best and truest parts of themselves for fear of being found out. But that was something he would have to learn to live with, and all things considered, it was a small price to pay to have a friend in his life the like of whom he'd never thought he would find.

They separated before reaching the church at the top of Main Street, Hugo standing firm on visiting the butcher's shop, where prices were high and his coupons would be required. He had decided on cottage pie for supper, followed by poached apples if the greengrocer had any available. Giving Tommy directions to purchase bread and vegetables, as well as a couple of Mr Hammond's best apples, Hugo prepared to do battle with Mr Fletcher over half a pound of his finest beef mince.

The operation successfully completed, and with the addition of a couple of kidneys for breakfast, Hugo popped into the general store and splurged on a tin of Bird's custard powder, feeling rather pleased. He met Tommy at the corner of the churchyard, and the two compared notes on their journey home.

"Nobody give you any trouble?" Hugo asked as he put away their purchases, pausing to admire the vibrant red and green of the Cox's apples Tommy had bought.

"Nothin' I can't handle," Tommy said, putting the kettle on to boil.

"What does that mean?" Hugo asked sharply. "Who said something?"

"Only one of them silly women." Tommy shrugged. "I don't take nobody serious who's wearin' cherries on her head."

Hugo snorted. He had a feeling he'd enjoy watching a confrontation between Tommy and Mrs Ponsonby.

"Shepherd's pie?" Tommy asked, looking at the ingredients Hugo was packing away.

"Close. Cottage."

"I never knew the difference," Tommy admitted.

"There isn't much. Shepherd's lamb, this is beef. That all right with you?"

Tommy beamed. "That sounds capital."

Hugo was unable to control the pleased pink blush staining his cheeks.

*****

They spent the afternoon in the kitchen, drinking endless cups of tea, which grew progressively weaker as the tea leaves in the pot lost their potency. Still, they eked out all the flavour they could before discarding them, both keenly aware of the meagre amount supplied by the ration.

As the sun set and dusk drew in, Hugo turned his thoughts to supper. He whistled softly under his breath as he retrieved the potatoes and carrots from the pantry and set them in the sink to wash and peel, placing a pan of dried peas in a pan to soak.

"Can I help?" Tommy asked, snaking his arms around Hugo's waist and resting his head on his shoulder to watch what he was doing.

"I thought you couldn't cook?" Hugo said with a laugh.

"I think I can peel carrots."

Hugo shook his head. "I'm all right," he said, smiling at Tommy's reflection in the window, the two of them illuminated against the liquid black glass. The hall light in his neighbour's house came on, and Hugo frowned. "You could get the blackouts, if you wouldn't mind? They're in the attic, to the left of the hatch."

"You still worried someone will see in?" Tommy asked quietly.

Hugo peeled a carrot with rather more vigour than was strictly necessary. "There's no telling who might be watching," he said at length. "We need to be careful."

Tommy nodded, releasing Hugo. "You're right," he admitted ruefully.

"It mightn't be forever," Hugo said, detecting something in Tommy's tone that gave him pause. Turning, he faced his friend.

"I know." Tommy gave Hugo a smile that didn't quite reach his eyes. "In the attic, on the left, you said?"

"That's right. The ladder's on the landing."

Tommy nodded. "I'll go get them, then."

Impulsively, he gave Hugo a quick kiss on the lips, turning and leaving the room before Hugo could respond. A few stray notes of a whistled tune reached Hugo as he continued peeling the vegetables, the same tune he'd been whistling, he realised: the tune they'd whistled to one another that day in the woods.

CHAPTER THIRTEEN

The house was too quiet, Hugo realised with a sudden sense of trepidation. He'd peeled and chopped the carrots, fried the beef mince with a spoonful of Bovril, added the peas, and boiled the potatoes. He'd taken his time, artfully arranging the mashed spuds over the mince, scratching the surface of the pie with a fork before adding a sparse handful of cheese. The last of his ration, but Tommy was worth it. Now their supper was in the oven, and Hugo realised Tommy should have come down from the attic long before.

Leaving the kitchen, he called Tommy's name into the hall. Silence answered. Hugo took the stairs two at a time, noted the ladder still leaning against the wall in the landing, the open door and neatly made bed in his mama's room. He descended, his boots clattering against the wooden treads either side of the thin strip of carpet running up the centre of the stairs. Tommy's coat was gone from the hook beside the front door. Hugo's heart sank.

He didn't need a note to tell him where his friend had gone. It seemed Tommy was determined to return to his cabin, to face down his murderous stalker alone. Looking at the clock on the parlour mantle, Hugo felt the first tendrils of fear claw down his spine. How long had Tommy been gone? What if the murderer had already caught up with him? Would he even defend himself, or did he truly believe he deserved to die for what he'd done?

Hugo forced himself to stop. Stop thinking, stop panicking. Tommy needed his help. The moment that thought occurred to him, Hugo's fear vanished, lost in the greater sense of having a purpose. If Tommy was going to be fool enough to go into the forest at night, Hugo would at least ensure he didn't have to go alone.

Mind made up, Hugo acted swiftly. He turned off the oven, pulled on his overcoat and flat cap, and opened the locked drawer of the bureau in the parlour. The gun was wrapped in soft cloth, the ammunition in a small, innocuous-looking waxed box next to it. Hugo lifted the weapon, the cold, heavy metal growing warm in his hot hands.

It was an Enfield No.2 revolver, standard service issue for the British Army. A handful had been distributed among the Home Guard and Hugo had somehow ended up with one, although he had only fired it once or twice in training. Hugo wasn't unfamiliar with guns—Puddledown was a country town, and most of the residents had a shotgun for keeping down vermin—but somehow the revolver seemed more dangerous, more menacing than his trusty Smith & Wesson.

Hugo opened the gun to load the chamber, his hands trembling just a fraction as he did so. Part of him felt the absurdity of his actions; he was a scholar, a man who felt remorse shooting rabbits, and here he was loading a revolver with the intention of pointing it at a living person. But then, Hugo reasoned as he closed the barrel, nothing stopped a man so readily as the sight of a gun. The sound of a shot alone was intimidation enough, and the murderer only had a knife, judging from the fact the victims had both been stabbed.

A floorboard creaked and Hugo sighed with relief and

laid down the gun as a sturdy arm snaked around his waist. Tommy must have stepped outside for a moment, or been in the bathroom when Hugo called. Now he would look a fool for panicking but at least that's all it was, an overreaction.

Cold metal bit into Hugo's throat, the blade of a large knife. He swallowed and felt his skin graze as his Adam's apple moved over the razor-edge. Dread seized him and he lashed out, his elbow connecting with stout ribs. A deep, masculine grunt sounded and the knife was pressed harder against his neck, until he felt the tickle of dripping blood. Immediately, Hugo stilled.

"Not so stupid, are yer?" the man pinning Hugo growled. A stranger, he noted with something that felt almost like relief. Tommy wasn't the killer, after all. "Yer jus' hold still now, or yer might find my hand slips."

Holding still would not be a problem. Hugo had always thought being scared stiff was a figure of speech, but he doubted he'd be able to move if he tried.

The man released Hugo's waist, keeping the knife pressed flush to his neck as he picked up the gun. Hugo heard the hammer click and the man pressed it between his shoulder blades as he withdrew the knife and retreated a short distance.

"W-What's this about?" Hugo asked tremulously. "I haven't got any money—"

"I don't want yer money!" the man snapped.

"M-My friend will be here soon. You'll get caught. You don't want to go to gaol for this."

"Yer *friend* left." The way he sneered the word chilled Hugo's blood. "Gone back 'ome to play the hero, no doubt. Thinks I'm going after 'im."

"Are you?" Hugo asked, a new fear surpassing the old—fear for Tommy.

The man snickered nastily. "All in good time."

Hugo's heart sank. Ever since the note had been pushed through his letterbox that morning, he'd known in his bones this was all about hurting Tommy. The groundskeeper probably thought he was doing right by his friend, getting away from Hugo so he wouldn't be harmed. Instead, he'd left Hugo alone and defenceless.

"The police are on to you," Hugo bluffed, turning to face his aggressor. "We took them the note you left."

"Liar." The man hissed the word. "You didn't go near the police station."

"So you have been following us." Hugo's tone was flat.

He contemplated the figure before him. There was something so... *wrong* about this man being the person to have done all the terrible things Hugo knew he had. He looked so innocuous, with his grey hair and thick glasses, like a harmless grandfather. Or perhaps not so harmless, for he was a head taller than Hugo, at least, and he didn't move like an old man. His steps were brisk and purposeful, and he held himself without succumbing to stooping as tall people often did. He might be twice Hugo's age, but Hugo suspected he was as robust as he had ever been.

"What do you want?" Hugo demanded. "If you're going to kill me, then do it. Get it over with!"

"Not so fast." The man smiled, a terrible baring of yellowed teeth. Hugo's lip curled to see it. "Tommy likes yer. I saw that last night. That makes you useful."

Hugo blanched. "Whatever you thought you saw—"

"I *know*," the man sneered. "I've met your sort before. Filthy creatures." He spat a wet gob on the floor and Hugo watched with revulsion as it soaked into his carpet. "It don't surprise me what 'e gets up to—but you. You I thought better of. Reckoned 'e were only fooling around with that lad from the 'otel. Then again, what do men like you know of loyalty?"

Hugo fought to keep his expression neutral, but his captor's nasty laugh said he'd been unsuccessful. Hugo couldn't deny it hurt, having his worst suspicions confirmed. Tommy was an attractive man, and Archie had been a fine-looking boy. No doubt he'd grown into a handsome youth. The sort of person who belonged with somebody like Tommy, who was clearly settling for second best where Hugo was concerned. He'd been visibly shaken by the discovery of Archie's body—and with good cause. Hugo realised, with a sinking heart, all Tommy had wanted from him was solace.

"If you know about Archie, then why do you think Tommy would care about me?" Hugo asked peevishly. "What did I ever do to you? I never even knew Bill Davies."

The man flinched as Hugo said the name. "Bill was my son!" he screamed, spittle flying, the cold malevolence of a moment earlier giving way to white-hot rage. "That good fer nothing little queer murdered my son, an he's going to pay for what 'e did. He took away the only thing what was good in my life, so I'm going to take everything what's good from 'im."

"So you're going to kill anyone he even passes a few words with?" Hugo asked, surprised and appalled. "You murdered an old woman because she asked him for gardening advice. You're insane!"

"Don't call me that!" the man shrieked, waving Hugo's revolver wildly. "I'm teaching that arrogant little shit a lesson he'll never forget. Tommy's going to suffer the way 'e made my Bill suffer, then he'll know how it feels to 'ave nothing in this world. I'll look 'im in the eye as the lights leave 'em, and I'll gladly follow 'im all the way to Hell."

Hugo sucked a breath. The man really was a lunatic. His eyes shone as he spoke, and it wasn't difficult to see he believed himself on some sort of righteous mission, exacting a terrible vengeance for his son's death. There was no reasoning with men like this.

"Move," the man growled, indicating the doorway with a jerk of the revolver.

"W-Where are we going?" Hugo asked.

The man looked at him like he was an idiot. "We're

going to pay Tommy a little visit," he sneered.

Hugo gulped and stepped forward, skirting the barrel of the revolver as he exited the room.

"Torch," the man growled, and Hugo obediently picked it up from the table beside the front door. "And no funny business. Yer jus' going for a walk. Try to run or shout and I'll put a bullet in yer back."

Hugo nodded to show he understood.

The street was dark, save the lights from the windows of the neighbouring houses. It was early evening, but the sun had long set, and Hugo supposed most families were sitting down to supper or listening to the wireless, going about their mundane, blameless lives, following the same routine, not knowing a murderer was right now stalking the very street on which they lived. The street they believed safe enough to leave their front doors unlatched and let their children play on unattended.

Hugo reached the end of the road and entered the country lane that circled the woods, cutting off onto an isolated track which would lead to the path towards Tommy's cabin. He lit his flashlight, the canopy of bare branches casting weird shadows on the ground as the light of a half-moon filtered through them. He kept the torch's beam low, his eyes on the dirt track through the sparse, brittle undergrowth, trying to ignore the creeping blackness of the forest closing in on either side.

The hairs on the back of his neck prickled with tension, his ears straining to pick up even the faintest sound. He felt the murder's eyes upon him, their beady stare boring holes into him as surely as any bullet. He was going to die tonight. He was going to let some stranger march him through the woods and put him down like an animal. The only reason he was still alive was because the madman behind him wanted to eke out the maximum impact from his death. The last thing Hugo was going to see on this good Earth was Tommy's stricken expression as he watched his lights go out. Then Tommy, too, would die, and there was nothing Hugo could do about it.

Tommy's cabin was half a mile or more into the woodland, and Hugo imagined the small clearing, a cheery lamp lit in the window, a fire stoked in the hearth. Hugo imagined evenings that could have been, the two of them sitting close under a blanket on the old horsehair sofa, watching flames dance in the fire and kissing until the embers died and it was time to go to bed.

Hugo's breath billowed before him in the still air, the cold nibbling his lips and ears and eyelids. He pulled his flat cap lower over his head, his chin tucked into his upturned collar, all his senses attuned to the slow, steady tramp of footsteps keeping time with his own.

His initial terror worn off, Hugo's analytical mind started whirring. If he was going to die, the least he could do was make an effort to save Tommy. A revolver was no deterrent if he was going to be shot anyway, and the sound would serve as a warning if nothing else. Perhaps someone in one of the outlying cottages would hear it and raise the alarm. Perhaps he would by some miracle manage to get away. He had to at least try.

He tripped on a root and stumbled, the torchlight veering like the lights of a drunken ship lost at sea. The man behind him cursed and sped up, the blunt muzzle of the gun shoved between his shoulder blades, forcing him onward. Hugo regained his footing and continued at a brisker pace. It was strange, but the man holding him at gunpoint didn't look like a murderer. Not that Hugo was sure what a murderer was supposed to look like. Tommy had made it plain enough most of the fellows Hugo brushed shoulders with had killed in their time. Somehow, however, that seemed different, not only because it was required of soldiers at war, but because Tommy's victims were chosen by Fate alone, killed without malice, a simple act of self-preservation. War was a time for doing or dying. Soldiers didn't select their victims ahead of time and hunt them down like foxes in a hole.

This man, this stranger—he was insane, Hugo felt sure. No person, possessed of all their faculties, could knife a defenceless old woman in the chest or slit a young man's throat. The sight of Mrs Fairchild's body had been enough to haunt Hugo for days after. To be responsible for creating such a terrible corpse was unthinkable.

He had to get away, and with his captor hard on his heels following his stumble, Hugo knew he'd never have a better chance. Offering up a silent prayer, Hugo feigned another slip. The man reacted immediately, grasping Hugo by the neck of his jacket and hauling him upright. Hugo used the motion to turn and swing wildly with his torch. It connected hard against the man's head, he let out a guttural grunt and released Hugo's coat.

Hugo ran.

He didn't know the forest well enough to know where he was going, but he ran nonetheless. Spying a side-path, Hugo dived into it, forcing his way through clawing branches and snagging undergrowth, hearing only a bellow of frustration echoing behind him, and the crashing sound of his own desperate escape. He saw malevolent intent in every dark shadow, every gently stirring frond of grey-brown bracken. He hastened faster along the path, blood rushing in his ears, the pounding of his heart like the drum of footsteps keeping time with his own.

Hugo swallowed his panic with difficulty. He was breathing hard, ragged breaths through open lips and parted teeth, animalistic, snarling. Sweat soaked his skin, cold and clammy where the heavy night air seeped under his coat and through his sensible layers. The silence of the forest closed in, encompassing him until it felt like his ears were underwater, even the sound of his own breaths coming muffled and weirdly distorted.

How could Tommy stand living out here? How could he possibly feel safe in this unholy wood, surrounded by terrible shadows and otherworldly shapes? Where was the welcoming light of his cabin? How many more twists and turns along this infernal path must Hugo take before he reached the sanctuary of brightness and warmth, of locked doors and loving arms?

Loud crashing in the undergrowth behind him told Hugo his pursuer was catching up. He staggered off the path and into the woods, finally coming to a halt several feet farther into the forest. He stood trembling, trying desperately to control his panicked breaths. The sound of the madman's advance slowed, the beam of the torch visible through the trees as the man sought him out. Hugo knew he needed to be as still and silent as the forest, but he felt sure the rapid drum of his heart must be audible over the sound of the gently stirring trees.

The tramp of footsteps came closer, heavy and purposeful. The sickly beam of the torch shone through the branches, casting weird shadows. Hugo crouched lower behind his tree and wished himself invisible. A twig cracked farther along the path, and Hugo released a relieved breath. The torchlight immediately swung around, fixing on him with unerring accuracy, then the silence of the night was broken by the deafening retort of the gun.

CHAPTER FOURTEEN

The bark of the tree behind which Hugo was hiding shattered, large splinters flying into his face. Hugo barely registered that the bullet had missed him before he was running, crashing through the forest full-pelt, the whites of his eyes rolling as he looked back, fully expecting to see the madman bearing down upon him. His breath caught in his lungs, his calves burnt, and he sobbed in terror, racing blindly on through the darkness.

Hugo's mad rush came to an abrupt halt as he tripped, turning his ankle and tumbling in a heavy heap, knocking the breath from his lungs.

More twigs cracked, closer and louder, unmistakably the sound of a large body emerging from the woods onto the path a short distance behind the spot where Hugo lay. His ankle throbbed, and the scald across his fingers stung. He could feel all the places he'd connected with the floor when he fell, and he knew he'd be covered in scrapes and bruises come morning.

If he survived until morning.

Hugo choked on a sob as he scrambled to stand, cursing as his ankle gave way and he fell again with a whimper, his cap lost and coat torn, hands sore and heart pounding in his chest. A low, throaty chuckle made the hairs on the back of his neck stand on end, the sound rippling down his spine and pooling in his belly. Hugo fought for control of his trembling limbs as worn work boots strode into view, their pace leisurely, their owner in no hurry now his quarry was down.

Hugo watched in horror as the man came to a stop before him, the dark muzzle of the gun pointed directly at his face, the torchlight blinding his eyes. Hugo imagined Tommy hearing the shot, discovering his body, and he wondered if his friend would cry for him, or if they were both destined to die out here in the woods on this cold and lonely night. He wondered if it hurt, if he would feel the moment his soul was ripped from his body and Hugo Arnold Wainwright ceased to exist, became nothing more than food for worms. It wasn't fair. There was so much he had wanted to do.

"On yer feet," the man growled.

Hugo lay cringing in the dirt. All the fight had gone out of him and he wasn't sure he could stand on his injured ankle, no matter what he was threatened with. The man kicked him in the ribs, then again in the gut, and Hugo doubled up, curling in on himself as he gasped and gagged.

"Git up," the man growled. "Or there's more where that came from."

Hastily, Hugo scrambled to his feet. His ankle twinged as he put weight on it, and he almost fell again. *Maybe Tommy heard the gunshot*, he thought desperately. Maybe his friend would go for help or come to his rescue. His ears rang as his captor moved behind him, the muzzle of the gun pressed between his shoulder blades once more, forcing him to limp on through the woods.

The walk to Tommy's cabin was excruciating. Tears stung Hugo's eyes as he dragged his twisted ankle, the torchlight throwing his shadow before him in stark relief, blocking his view of the path, the blunt muzzle of the gun prodding between his shoulder blades every time he stumbled or slowed.

After what seemed an eternity, Hugo spied a light through the trees that could only be from Tommy's window. His gut rolled with a queasy combination of fear and joy, knowing Tommy was the man's ultimate quarry but hoping against hope his friend had heard the gunshot and fetched help. Even Jimmy Cooper's arrogant face would be a welcome sight.

Hugo entered the clearing, his heart in his mouth. Tommy's window was uncovered, the light he had seen coming from a lamp placed on the sill before it. The door was open, Tommy's frame a dark silhouette in the entrance.

"Hugo?" Tommy took half a step forward, but Hugo raised his hand to hold him back. The concern in Tommy's voice melted to grim determination as he asked, "Where is he?"

"I ain't no fool," the man called from the shadows at the edge of the clearing. Hugo didn't know when he'd switched off the torch, but in the gloomy woods, without a light to betray his whereabouts, he could have been anywhere. "I've got a gun trained on yer friend, 'ere, so don't take another step closer if you don't want 'im to get hurt."

"Who are you?" Tommy snapped. "What's this all about?"

"You know what," the man growled.

"Bill? I don't know what you think you know—"

"He's his father," Hugo said.

Tommy's expression wiped blank with shock. "Reg?" he asked tentatively. "Reg Davies?"

The man chuckled, and Hugo's skin crawled. "You think you're smart, don't yer? I've been following you, I've followed you since London, biding my time. I was going to kill yer right here. I let myself in, stood over you while yer slept like a baby. Never even knew I was there. I was going to slit yer throat right then, get it over with, until I realised it'd be too good for the likes of you."

"I don't know what you think you know—"

"I know you killed him!" Hugo winced at the fury and raw pain in the man's voice. "He was my son, and you killed him!"

"Archie Bucket was somebody's son," Tommy said coldly. "That didn't stop you from slaughterin' him like a pig. Eighteen, he was, an' his ma and sister depended on him. Did you know that? Do you even care?"

"That's too bad," the man said. "You made my boy suffer. Now I'll make you suffer the same. I want people to look at you and know what you are, Thomas Granger. A worthless murderer and a queer!"

"Your words don't frighten me," Tommy said, his voice as cold as ice and steady as a rock. "I already know what I am."

"You disgust me," Reg hissed. "The company you keep, the things you get up to. You ain't got no shame."

Tommy shrugged, affecting an air of nonchalance Hugo could only assume was feigned. He felt like passing out, welcoming the cold embrace of the earth and letting this awful confrontation slip away into the darkness of oblivion.

"You're right," Tommy said. "I'm completely shameless. I like to suck cock. Get on my knees an' grovel on it. I never sucked Bill's, he weren't into that sort of thing. So I don't see how it matters to you."

Hugo flushed with embarrassment and humiliation at Tommy's words, even as Reg spat out a curse.

"I can tell you why, if you like," Tommy continued. "Isn't that what you really want to know? Why I killed him."

Reg sucked a sharp breath. "You won't even deny you done it?"

"Why should I?" Tommy countered. "It seems you already know."

"Weren't as careful as yer thought," Reg said, gloating.

"'Died of Wounds,' that's what the telegram said. I believed it, too, for a while. But you was seen, Thomas Granger. Some chap witnessed what you done and wrote me as soon as 'e was able. Said he watched you snuff Bill's lights out with 'is own eyes. I'm only sorry he never lived long enough for me to thank 'im for writing that note."

"How did you find me?" Tommy asked.

"It took some time." There was malevolent glee in Reg's voice. "Had to wait 'til the war was over, see. Yer sergeant gave me yer mam's address, but she weren't there no more, was she? So I went up to Scarborough, I did. Spoke to yer mam and yer sister and 'er chap." He whistled, long and low. "Doesn't like you much, does 'e, the good reverend? Said there'd been trouble, didn't want your sort around. Wasn't sure what he meant at first. Figured you 'adn't told 'im you was a low-down, murdering bastard. Gave me an address in London, 'e did, and I soon learnt the truth about the sort of man you are."

"Bill was my friend," Tommy said, a touch of steel in his voice. "He knew the sort of man I was—he knew everything—an' he was my friend anyway. Felt like the only friend I had, most days. I never wanted anythin' to harm him."

Hugo's heart ached at the plaintive note on which Tommy ended. He'd have given anything to be able to stop his ears so he didn't have to listen to any more shameful details. Or else go to Tommy, take him in his arms and offer a measure of comfort for all he'd been through.

"You killed 'im!" Reg screamed. "You weren't no friend to my son. You was 'is murderer!"

"He was dying!" Tommy shouted back, his voice breaking. "He was hit in the chest an' he wasn't goin' to make it. I didn't want the Germans gettin' to him."

"Lies!" Reg cried, advancing angrily from his hiding place at the edge of the trees.

"It's the truth." Tommy lifted his arms, then dropped

them in a helpless gesture. "I'd have changed places with him in a heartbeat," he said sadly. "Bill deserved to live an' I didn't, I know that. There ain't nothin' you can do to make me feel worse about it than I already do."

"Now see here," Hugo said, overcome with an urgent need to correct Tommy. The thought of his friend dying sent a shock through him, greater even than the fear of his own death.

A strong hand grasped Hugo's hair, wrenching his head back until he choked on the rest of his words.

"What about 'im?" Reg asked, his voice hissing as he touched the cold barrel of the gun to Hugo's temple. "Would yer take his place?"

"Leave him out of this!" Tommy snapped. He took a hasty step forward but halted as Reg dragged Hugo back. "He's a good man. He had nothin' to do with any of it!"

"I saw you," Reg whispered directly into Hugo's ear, so close Hugo could smell the foulness of his breath. "I saw what you did, right before your front window like a pair of brazen perverts. You should be shot, the lot of yer." He spat on the floor to the side of Hugo's foot, the gob landing with a sickly wet sound.

Hugo cringed. Wasn't this what he'd been afraid of all his life? Of being seen, found out, and branded a degenerate? His very first kiss—clumsy, confused thing that it was—being used to sign his death sentence.

A thousand regrets welled in his breast, yet when he looked at Tommy, they all melted away. Men like Reg could think what they liked—say what they liked—Hugo had spent far too long being ashamed of who he was. They wouldn't get to him again. He knew his feelings for Tommy came from the best part of himself, his ability to give and receive love, to put another first, to support and defend him. Those were the most natural, most human instincts Hugo possessed. He wouldn't suppress them again for anyone.

"You don't scare me," Hugo said. "What are you? Just

a coward who kills old women and young boys. I hope they haunt you. I hope you see their faces when you close your eyes. I hope you hear them screaming and you can't sleep for guilt over what you did."

"Shut up," Reg snapped, wrenching Hugo's hair until his whole scalp felt as though it had been lit on fire.

"What would Bill say, Reg?" Hugo cried. "What would your son say if he could see you now?"

"Ask 'im!" Reg gesticulated wildly at Tommy, who had taken another step closer, but retreated as the gun was turned on him. "My son is gone, and it's all 'is fault!"

"Listen to what he was telling you," Hugo implored. "Bill was his best friend. Tommy tried to help him the only way he knew how."

"He murdered 'im!" Reg screamed, spittle flying, thrusting Hugo to the ground.

"Would you rather the Germans had got him?" Hugo asked. "Bill was *dying*, Reg. There was nothing Tommy could do to prevent it." He staggered to his feet, wincing as he put his weight on his twisted ankle, but it didn't feel broken. Not that Hugo had ever broken a bone to compare the pain. He merely prayed it continued to hold as he faced Reg, standing between the murderer and his real quarry.

Reg's eyes were wild, the whites rolling as he turned on Hugo. "What do you know about it?" he demanded. "Were you there? Did you see it? Or are you taking a murderer's word for how 'e killed my son?"

"So kill me," Tommy said, crossing the clearing to Hugo's side. "You've got a gun, an' I won't put up a fight. If you think it will help, kill me for what I've done. Lord knows, I deserve it."

"No!" Hugo grabbed Tommy and tried to push him aside, but the compact groundskeeper was surprisingly strong. "Tommy, *no*." Hugo looked straight into his liquid black eyes. "I won't let you do this."

Tommy smiled sadly and touched Hugo's cheek. "I'm

sorry I involved you in this."

"You'll have to kill us both," Hugo said to Reg. "Because I won't let you get away with this. I'll go to the police, I'll testify. I don't care what you tell them about me."

"Isn't that touching?" Reg sneered, his voice dripping derision. "Mebbe I don't want to kill 'im. Mebbe I want to see him suffer." He flashed Tommy a look so full of malevolence as to be barely human. "Your sort don't have sons, so you'll never know what was taken from me. But you"—he jabbed the gun towards Hugo—"you he cares for. He'd miss you if you were gone."

The blood left Hugo's face as he realised what Reg was going to do.

"I knew Bill," Tommy said, his voice wavering only slightly as he tried to get Reg's attention. "He were a good man. The best of men. He took pity on a poor bugger like me an' allowed me to call him friend."

"My son would never be friends with the likes of *you*." Reg spat the word furiously.

"He told me about you," Tommy continued as though Reg hadn't spoken. "Just you an' him, wasn't it? His ma died when he was still in school. Consumption. You sent him away to the seaside. He lived with his cousins near Brighton. He always spoke of his dad, his old man. How you'd always done your best by him, always wanted him to do well."

Tommy advanced so slowly even Hugo was barely aware of the movement. "An' there was a girl, Florence. Said you always thought her name was too high an' mighty, but he loved her an' he wanted to marry her once the war was over. He showed me a photograph, took it everywhere with him. Said he knew, whatever happened, she'd be all right, because you'd look out for her if he were gone." Tommy's mouth twisted in a bitter smile. "I used to tell him not to talk like that."

"So you overheard some things," Reg muttered. "It

don't mean nothin'." He sounded confident, but his face was haunted by doubt.

"An' me." Tommy swallowed audibly. "He wanted me to look after myself, too. Said I deserved better than what I thought I did, an'... an' I needed to respect myself more. He knew I weren't never gettin' married, but he said once he hoped I found myself someone, a 'nice chap,' he said, so I could know what it was he felt for his Flo. He said it weren't nobody's business but my own, an' he hoped I wound up somewhere folk felt the same way as he did about those things."

"That was your son," Hugo said, taking over when Tommy's voice broke. "He was a good man, Reg, and a good friend to Tommy. But he was hit, he was dying, and Tommy knew he couldn't save him. What would you have done?"

Reg faltered, his eyes wet with unshed tears. For the briefest moment, Hugo felt sorry for the man. He'd seen enough parents grieve for their children, strapping sons cruelly cut down in the prime of life, fighting a war their fathers had given their lives to prevent. Reg was looking for somebody to blame, to hold accountable for Bill's death. Hitler and Germany, Chamberlain and the government, they were abstracts from the wireless, names without faces. Reg wanted to look into the eyes of the man he blamed for his son's death and show him what he'd done. Hugo cursed the interfering soldier who'd seen and told but half a story.

"He was my boy," Reg said sadly. "My beautiful boy."

"I know." Tommy nodded. "I miss him, too."

Reg looked at Tommy, his features hardening as anger swelled once more to the surface. "It should have been you," he snarled. "Why did Bill 'ave to die, but you didn't? Were you a coward, is that it? Did Bill take a bullet protecting your yellow hide?"

"It was a sniper!" Tommy protested, pulling Hugo back with him as Reg advanced. "He could have got any of us, but he got Bill. I don't know why. I wish with everythin' I've got he hadn't."

"Bill wouldn't want this," Hugo said, his voice rising with alarm as Reg backed them towards the cabin. The moonlight glinted in the waves of his grey hair, gunmetal grey in the darkness.

"You don't know what my son would want," Reg snarled, pointing the gun straight into Hugo's face.

Hugo closed his eyes, not wanting to see the trigger pulled, the bullet barrelling towards his head in a blinding explosion that would be his last conscious memory of the world. Instead, he thought of Tommy, of the way the groundskeeper's face lit up at a joke, the way his hands moved as he smoked a cigarette. The feel of his lips and taste of his mouth. The memories were but beggar's scraps of comfort, but they were the best Hugo had.

Beside him, Tommy bellowed, outright fear in his voice, but Hugo was immune to it, was immune to everything but the drumming of his heart and the trickle of hot urine running down his inside leg, giving the lie to his composed appearance.

Somebody shoved him, his weight landed on his twisted ankle, pain shot through his leg, and Hugo fell with a deafening bang which wasn't, he realised a moment later, the sound of his fall at all, but a gunshot ripping through the night and leaving silence in its wake.

In that instant, Hugo was aware of everything: of the cold, hard-packed earth beneath his cheek, small lumps of gravel digging into his skin. Of the pain in his ankle, throbbing, acute, and the slow burn of grazed palms. He felt each ragged breath he took like a miracle, telling him he was still alive. Even the wet patch of his corduroys sticking to his leg was received as welcome proof he wasn't dead.

The sound of Tommy's laboured breathing hit Hugo like a pail of cold water, and he opened his eyes to see his friend looking down at him, concern written in every line

THE DEAD PAST

of his face.

"Are you hurt?" Tommy asked, running his hands over Hugo's face and chest and arms.

"I'm all right." Hugo pushed Tommy away and forced himself to sit upright. "What happened?"

But Tommy wasn't listening. The moment he was satisfied Hugo wasn't seriously injured, he rose from his squatting position, Hugo's revolver clutched tightly in his hand. His heart in his mouth, Hugo watched Tommy level the gun at Reg.

"Do it," Reg said, standing stock still a few paces from them. There was a small cut on his cheekbone, near his eye, where Hugo concluded Tommy had punched him, forcing him to drop the gun. "Come on, yer coward. Do it! Shoot me!"

The gun trembled in Tommy's hand, his knuckles white around the handle. Slowly, deliberately, he cocked the weapon.

"I could," Tommy said softly. "I could end you right here an' now. You deserve it for what you've done."

Hugo held his breath, not daring to move or do anything to break the spell cast over the forest clearing. From his position he could see into the cabin through the open door, see Tommy's uneven table and the corner of his horsehair sofa, the brightly coloured blanket folded into a neat square across the back. So homely, it looked. All Hugo wanted was to crawl inside and hold Tommy to him, listen to the steady, reassuring beat of his heart as he fell asleep. It seemed inconceivable that his gentle, sweet-natured friend was pointing a gun at a man's head and considering ending his life.

"What are you waiting for?" Reg demanded. "Too chickenshit, is that it? Not brave enough to kill a man unless he can't fight back?"

Tommy tightened his grip on the trigger, and Hugo winced. Reg deserved it, Hugo knew he did, but he didn't want to watch Tommy kill him in cold blood.

"I'm brave enough," Tommy growled. "But I won't."

He lowered the gun, and Hugo released the breath he'd been holding. Tommy caught his eye and gave him a brief smile, barely a twitch at the corner of his mouth, but Hugo took heart from the gesture. His Tommy wasn't a murderer.

"I'm turning you in," Tommy said. "You'll pay for what you've done in a court of law. P'raps they'll take pity on an old man an' won't hang you."

"I'll take you down with me," Reg snarled. "I'll tell 'em everything."

"Go ahead." Tommy shrugged. "You think they'll take a murderer's word over the man who turned him in?"

Reg's face twisted, impotent fury and anguish and a grim sort of determination that made Hugo freeze in fear.

"Wait—don't!"

Tommy threw himself forward just as Hugo saw the wicked-looking blade in Reg's hand. He wanted to close his eyes, but he found himself transfixed, unable to look away as Reg plunged the knife into his own chest, doubling over across the hilt, around which blood began to flow, a trail of black tar down his chest and hands.

Reg fell to his knees as Tommy reached him, emitting a low groan that Hugo knew would haunt him to his dying day. Tommy stood impotently over the old man, seemingly scared to touch him as he slumped slowly to the floor.

The last thing Hugo saw was Tommy's eyes, fathomless black and shining in the low light, tears finally flowing down his cheeks, before darkness descended and Hugo collapsed into the welcoming arms of oblivion.

EPILOGUE

It took Reg a long time to die. Tommy had run all the way to town to fetch help while Hugo, barely able to walk on his twisted ankle, waited with the dying man, grief and a sickening sense of impatience rushing over him as he watched him suffer through his self-inflicted injury. Hugo had learnt some basic first aid during his time with the Home Guard, but a stab wound in the chest was beyond his ability to treat. He had helplessly watched Reg's eyes grow glassy as he gargled on blood and air, but by the time Tommy returned, accompanied by the doctor and a police constable, the gargling had long since stopped.

Tommy helped Hugo up and had all but carried him into the cabin. He washed Reg's blood from Hugo's shaking hands and stole a brief, chaste kiss while the constable and the doctor were still distracted by the body lying on the ground outside.

The constable had wanted a statement, but Hugo found his words failed him. Always so articulate, he was barely coherent as he struggled to marshal his thoughts to answer the policeman's questions. Such simple questions, they seemed, yet the answers eluded him. All stories must have a beginning, a middle, and an end, but Hugo's thoughts were jumbled and he couldn't assemble a linear narrative of what he had seen. Afraid and bewildered, he had clung shamelessly to Tommy—the one constant in the swirling fog of his mind—until at last Tommy had refused to allow Hugo to be questioned further.

Doctor Neal had checked him over, Hugo remembered. He was a jolly sort of chap, even under circumstances such as he found himself that night. He declared Hugo's ankle sprained, his cuts superficial, and his mind shocked. A tot of brandy and a good night's sleep were his prescription, although when Tommy finally got Hugo back to his house, they near finished the bottle before blessed sleep would come.

Inspector Owens arrived at Ferndale promptly at nine the next morning and for once Hugo was pleased to see him, the interview a much easier ordeal than Tommy's blunt, perceptive questioning. Indeed, in the fortnight since, Hugo had been somewhat avoiding his friend. The man knew too much, had seen too much, had witnessed Hugo's cowardice, his inability to fight in defence of his life, or to even control his bladder. Were it not for Tommy, Hugo knew he would undoubtedly be dead, gunned down in the woods, his corpse left to rot in its own waste.

Hugo was also intensely embarrassed by the details of Tommy's past that had been revealed during the confrontation. He had known the facts surrounding Tommy's nature and Bill's death, but hearing the frank and explicit truth, told in obscene words, had been too much for poor Hugo to bear. The graphic pictures Tommy had painted were never far from Hugo's mind, as arousing as they were shocking, for now Hugo had some idea of what, exactly, Tommy had wanted from him, and his inside cheek grew bloody and ragged from the frequency with which he bit it.

Finally, Tommy took matters into his own hands, calling on Hugo at home one afternoon two weeks after they had last parted.

"Wasn't sure you'd want to see me," Tommy admitted after Hugo let him in and they'd settled at the kitchen table, two steaming mugs of tea between them.

"I meant to call on you," Hugo said. "I looked for you in the town."

"Been avoidin' it." Tommy sipped his tea and grimaced. "Can't bring myself to face those women."

"But they know you're innocent, now," Hugo pointed out. While only they knew all the details of what had happened that night in the woods, enough information had been released by the police to the local press that the reporters, used to dealing with secondhand news from farther afield, had had a field day, splashing the front pages with lurid accounts of what had transpired.

Reg Davies had been a sick man, diagnosed with cancer of the lungs and not predicted to last out the year. That detail was enough for the Chief of Police to write the murders off as the acts of a desperate man bound and determined to punish Tommy for surviving the war when his son had not. Inspector Owens seemed less satisfied with such a convenient explanation, but faced with silence from Hugo and Tommy, and pressure from his superior to put the case to bed, he had reluctantly declared the investigation into the matter closed.

"They don't care I'm innocent," Tommy grumbled. "It won't change their opinion of me, an' all they want is gossip."

Hugo nodded, knowing Tommy's words were true. He had been avoiding Main Street for the same reason. Indeed, he'd barely left his house, even after his ankle had healed well enough to permit him longer walks. Outside of Aunt Rose, he'd sought nobody's company.

The old woman had been a great comfort. Although Hugo couldn't discuss everything that troubled him, for fear of the damage the shock could do her, he had at least been able to unburden the majority of the details of their confrontation with Reg onto a sympathetic audience. Rose had shouldered that burden admirably, told Hugo to put the unfortunate incident behind him, and encouraged him to renew his friendship with Tommy. Advice he had failed to take, for how could Rose possibly understand the nature of their friendship or the terrible sins Hugo was struggling so valiantly to resist?

And now Tommy was here before him, looking as handsome as Hugo had ever seen him. He had forgotten, during their separation, the precise colour of Tommy's dark eyes, the sensuous curve of his lips, the way his long lashes fanned over his high cheekbones as he studiously avoided meeting Hugo's gaze. The soft, "I've missed you," was said unthinkingly, but once the words were out, Hugo found them to be true.

Tommy looked up, a pleased smile on his face. "Did you really?" he asked, almost shyly.

Hugo nodded.

Tommy's cheeks pinked. "Me, too. I missed you, that is."

"I, I did mean to call on you," Hugo said, keen for Tommy to believe him.

"S'all right." Tommy waved his hand, a thin trail of smoke from his freshly lit cigarette charting the movement before swirling and drifting away. "You don't have to explain. You're a busy man—"

"No." Hugo swallowed hard, but he wouldn't let Tommy make his excuses for him. "No, that wasn't it. Truthfully, I was afraid."

Tommy's eyes widened. "Of what?" he asked cautiously.

Hugo swallowed again. "I haven't been back in the woods since," he admitted, blushing for shame at his cowardice. His whole life he'd lived in Puddledown, and he'd never been scared to go anywhere. One dark night in the forest had obliterated all his earlier experiences and, irrational though he knew it was with Reg Davies dead and gone, the idea of revisiting the clearing outside Tommy's cabin struck terror in Hugo's heart.

"Oh. *Oh.*" Tommy's eyes widened still further as the meaning of Hugo's words became clear.

"How do you do it?" Hugo asked urgently. "How did you go back there—sleep there—knowing what happened?"

Tommy ran a hand over the back of his head, looking suddenly uncomfortable and unsure. He took a long drag of his cigarette, blowing the smoke away from Hugo in a neat plume before answering. "I had to," he eventually said, shrugging helplessly. "It ain't like I had somewhere else to go."

"You could have stayed here," Hugo said, a little wounded Tommy hadn't asked.

"I didn't think that were a good idea." Tommy grimaced. "Not with me an' you—" He broke off, gesturing between them for Hugo to fill in the blanks.

"You could have had the spare room."

"I didn't *want* the spare room," Tommy said fiercely. "Don't you see, Hugo, that's the problem. You ain't ready for what I want."

Hugo coloured anew as a vision rose before him, one which had haunted his dreams with alarming frequency: Tommy, on his knees, unfastening the buttons of Hugo's trousers—

"See, that right there." Tommy thumped the table. "How much do you know, Hugo?"

Hugo cringed as Tommy stubbed his cigarette and leant forward, examining him with dark-eyed intensity.

"Lemme guess," Tommy said softly. "You know what you've read about in newspapers—which is nothin'—an' mebbe one or two o' them fancy books of yours. You know what folk call men like us, but you don't imagine bein' that sort yourself. Mebbe you saw somethin' between a couple of farmhands in a barn, or some of the fellows at school. P'raps they told you somethin'. An' you blushed that pretty blush o' yours an' closed your eyes an' ears to it, an' tried not to notice when some fellow caught your eye, pretended not to remember what you dreamt about when you dreamt of him. Am I right, Hugo?"

Hugo watched with a sense of foreboding as Tommy slowly, deliberately, reached across the table and brushed the inside of his wrist with his fingertips, sending a delicious shiver racing down his spine.

"No." He shook his head, the movement feeling strangely detached, like he was moving underwater. Still, he faced Tommy squarely as he answered. "I never pretended I couldn't remember," he said firmly. "I know who I am, Tommy—what I am—and I know what people think of men like me. I-I've always been honest with myself about that."

Tommy sat back, his eyebrows lifting in surprise, but Hugo didn't think it entirely his imagination Tommy also seemed impressed.

"You know I've never acted on it," he said in a rush, the words tumbling out now he'd started speaking. "You're right. I don't know much of anything about that side of things. I never saw anything, although some of the boys at school made jokes." He fought the heat rising in his cheeks as he struggled to continue. "The truth is, you're the first man I've known who was prepared to admit who he is, and I feel safe talking to you. I've never had that before."

Tommy grimaced sympathetically and patted the back of Hugo's hand.

"I don't want your pity." Hugo snatched his hand away, scowling as a wash of shame ran over him. The last thing he wanted was for Tommy to hear his painful confession, only to pity him for it.

Tommy smiled. "I don't pity you," he said, his tone making clear he was speaking the truth. "Honest, I don't."

"Then don't think differently about me," Hugo said. "The other night"—he swallowed hard—"what you wanted.... I could still, I mean, we could...." He made a frustrated sound, tears pricking his eyes for shame at what he was saying, and the deeper shame of being unable to say it. He was a grown man, reduced to a nervous wreck by a handful of words. How would he possibly find it within himself to do what he so desperately wanted to do if he couldn't even articulate his desires?

"Steady on." Tommy laughed nervously. "Don't do yourself an injury on my account. Some folks can't say it, is all. I reckon you're that type."

Hugo nodded miserably.

"I can go slow," Tommy said. "Teach you what you want to learn. I like you, Hugo. I want to go slow with you."

"You mean like courting?"

Tommy laughed, a light, musical sound. "If that's how you want to put it." He smiled, suddenly bashful. "I'll court you, Hugo Wainwright, if you'd like me to."

Hugo looked away as Tommy rose and rounded the table, his movements fluid, languid, like a sleek tabby closing in on a mouse. His breath caught as Tommy took his hand and bowed low to kiss the inside of his wrist, sending a shiver through him.

"Oh yes." Tommy smiled a slow, satisfied smile. "You an' me, Hugo. We're going to have the time of our lives. Just you wait an' see."

ABOUT THE AUTHOR

Born in Liverpool, Kate Aaron is a bestselling author of the #1 LGBT romances *What He Wants, Ace, The Slave*, and other works.

Kate swapped the North West for the Midwest in October 2015 and married award-winning author AJ Rose. Together they plan to take over the world.

KateAaron.com

Printed in Poland
by Amazon Fulfillment
Poland Sp. z o.o., Wrocław